By the Light of My Father's Smile

—

A Story of Requited Love, Crossing Over,
and the Sexual Healing of the Soul

Alice Walker

By the Light of My Father's Smile

A Novel

RANDOM HOUSE

NEW YORK

Copyright © 1998 by Alice Walker

All rights reserved under International and Pan-American
Copyright Conventions. Published in the United States by Random
House, Inc., New York, and simultaneously in Canada by
Random House of Canada Limited, Toronto.

Library of Congress Cataloging-in-Publication Data
Walker, Alice
By the light of my father's smile : a novel / Alice Walker
p.   cm.
ISBN 0-375-50152-5
I. Title.
PS3573.A425B9   1998   813'.54—dc21   98-5464

Random House Website Address: www.randomhouse.com
Manufactured in the United States of America
4 6 8 9 7 5 3

Book design by J. K. Lambert

To you, victorious
        who taught me
        fuzz of peach
        wet of pear

light of owl
        shine of
        bear.

        This scandalous
        prayer of
a
        book
                        both remembrance
&
        offering.

&
in kinship with

        our
                insouciant
                fun-loving
                nonreading
relatives
                the delightful cousins
        Bonobo.

        *May Life be thanked
        for them.*

We should rise up and praise when we talk about what friendship is and love is and what lovers are about—this interpenetration of one another's souls by way of the body. That's so marvellous! I think angels are envious of humans because we have bodies; they don't, and love-making makes the angels flap their wings in envy. . . . Human sexuality is a mystical moment in the history of the Universe. All the angels and all the other beings come out to wonder at this.

—FATHER MATTHEW FOX

From *Natural Grace: Dialogues on Science and Spirituality*
Rupert Sheldrake and Matthew Fox

The reason people and angels hover around human sexuality is because it is a light source that has been kept in the dark.

—a.w.

Mama
help us
to help
you.

Mundo prayer

ANGELS

Angels

When she goes to the city she leaves me lounging in the swing underneath the oak tree. She visualizes me as a shadow, as her car zooms around the curves that take her rapidly down the mountain. She is listening to a music I have not heard in many years. At first I think it is Portuguese fado; then I realize it is flamenco, which is also characterized by passion and profound sadness. She moans along with the woman who is singing—wailing, really—her hands gripping the steering wheel to the plangent cries of the singer and the sobbing of violins. The momentum of her flight sets the old swing to rocking. Her car is old and black. It was another expression of my effort to contact her.

She was not even aware at the time of my death that she missed me. Poor child. She did not cry at my funeral. She was a stoic spectator. Her heart, she thought, was closed. I watched her looking down at me, the father who gave her life, with the passivity of one who has borne all she intends to bear. She did not even bother to smirk as platitudes about me—most of them absurd—filled the church around her. When an especially large falsehood was uttered—that I would never have hurt a fly, for instance—she merely closed her eyes. At the gravesite she clutched the arm of her Greek husband, with his hard curly hair and black mustache, and, leaning as if to whisper in his hairy ear, discreetly yawned.

She did not know of my sorrow, dying. Poor child. How could she know?

That night, eating a pomegranate seed by seed beside the fire, she did not miss me. She felt rather as if something heavy and dark, something she could never explain, had rolled away, off her soul. Shameless, curious, forsaken somehow, I watched her and the Greek husband, late into the night, make love.

The recent stirrings that intimated my presence began with her desire to know about angels. Where they come from in the imagination, why people in all cultures find it difficult if not impossible to live without them. Is the angel in the imagination a memory of a loved one who has died? Is the angel an earth spirit existing in its own right, touching us with the benign blessing and direction of Nature? Why was she dreaming of angels every night?

She and the Greek went to Kalimasa. This was before tourists exhausted the public Kalimasan spirit, and there, everywhere, in everyone's home, flew an angel. *Watti-tuus*, as they were called. Some of them were simply winged women, with a woman's hands and eyes and feet. But some were winged mermaids, their bronze scales dusted with gold. Some were white as apples; others as brown as shining earth. She was—my daughter, Susannah—enchanted.

The Greek, Petros, was charmed by her passion. I watched as he fed himself full meals from the store of her enthusiasm. She was radiant and sensual. I saw that first time in Kalimasa that she was, as a woman, someone I truly did not know.

Petros bought an angel for her, a *watti-tuu*, as a surprise. It was a dark-haired, dark-skinned, full-breasted woman, with a belly filled with small people, tiny houses, birds. Its wings were painted shimmering green. She laughed gaily, as she had as a child. She clapped her hands. Joy radiated from her eyes. This was the spirit I had not seen for decades. I recognized it, though. And drew near to it, as if to a fire. I saw her frown, suddenly, as if aware of my shadow, and I hastily and regretfully withdrew.

The second time she went to Kalimasa, Petros did not go. She had lost him back in the States. This time she traveled with a woman who dressed inappropriately for the culture, and wore her bathing suit all day long, and accepted motorcycle rides from the local village males, who were losing their modesty and learning to take whatever pleasure came their way from the shameless tourist women. This woman, though good in bed, so irritated my daughter that she remained in the guest house they shared, day after sultry day, a blue linen sheet drawn taut over her head.

But when she did venture out onto the two streets of the tiny village of Wodra, more touristed than she would have dreamed possible the last time she was there, she did so feeling there was something drawing her. Of course she did not know what it was.

Damp, perspiring, though it was only eight or nine in the morning, she found herself at a jeweler's.

The Kalimasans are famous for their graceful aesthetic sense. For their innate appreciation of balance and proportion. This sense of what is just right can be seen in their architecture, in their canals, in their waterfalls. Even in their hairstyles. It is often said by visitors that everything in their landscape, except the mountains that frame most villages like spectacular stage props, is artificially constructed, yet looks totally natural. The fineness of the Kalimasans' eye is pronounced in the jewelry and clothing they make.

The shop, like all the shops on that end of the street near the restaurant and the river, was quite small. Only a few feet deep, after you climbed three steep steps up from the road. There were four rows of trinkets: rings, bracelets, necklaces. Nothing costing more than fifty U.S. dollars. Susannah began to try on bracelets, the ones that are made of brass and look a hundred years old, though they might have been made yesterday. And then her eye fell on the ring she'd been looking for without knowing it. Black onyx, an oval shape. Its sides splashed with gold. Though, since the ring cost only eighteen dollars, perhaps the gold was something else. The ring fit her finger perfectly. Happily she paid the young Hindu shopkeeper, continued on her way through the village of Wodra, and was even inspired to go as far as the Elephant Walk, a mile and a half from the village, before giving in to the desire to return to the guest house.

"What is the meaning of this ring?" the woman asked at dinner, in the whining, bossy voice my daughter had come to dread.

"It is beautiful," said Susannah. She raised her hand to her cheek and rested it there. The light from the candle made the gold splashes beside the onyx glow red.

"I wanted to give you a ring for that finger," the woman pouted.

"But I have nine others," said my daughter. "All vacant."

"You know what I mean," said the woman. Her name was Pauline. Dressed in a billowy native "costume"—for indeed, the villagers themselves rarely wore their traditional clothing anymore—she seemed plump and steamy. I read her as someone cutthroat in her intention to have, as an adult, the childhood she missed as a child. I did not see how Susannah could bear her.

My daughter sipped her drink thoughtfully. "You are looking very lovely yourself, tonight," she said.

The woman was instantly distracted by this compliment, as my daughter knew she would be. She began to puff herself out, across the table. To look for her image in my daughter's eyes.

My daughter's dark eyes were wide open. Frank. She allowed them to be mirrors for Pauline. Behind them, of course, she was deep in thought.

Of what is she thinking? Certainly not of me. Perhaps she is thinking of the Greek husband who ran off with a blond airline hostess. Of his discovery that the woman's hair was as dark as his own, naturally. And of his complaint. Whatever a woman was, was never enough, or right enough, for him. They'd quarreled because she loved wearing high heels, which indeed made him look quite short, and she'd often remarked that his taste in clothes— he admired tweeds and plaids, which she associated with square-ness and recent immigration—was bad.

But maybe not.

The woman across from Susannah is flirting with the young boy who is the waiter. When he brings a tray on which there are flowers as well as satay, she finds a reason to brush his brown arm with her own. The heady scent she wears rises full-blown into the sultry heat. All around her tension builds. She is the kind of woman who could provoke rain.

Later in the night, to show my daughter that she is indeed de-sirable, she and the young waiter will stand entwined in the shadow of the giant banana tree just off the wide, plant-filled ve-randah. My daughter will hear the sultry rustle of the woman's clothes. The pitiful, hopeful breathing of the young boy. Nothing will come of it, she knows. Pauline is too afraid of germs. Except in fantasy, she is also sexually indifferent to males.

Boys in Kalimasa still, for the most part, look innocent to Su-sannah. She imagines them as her sons. Their wide, dark eyes, easily perplexed, enchanted her. Their shy speech, in an English carefully learned. It disturbed and hurt her to see, over the years of her many visits, the first signs of envy creep into their dark eyes.

Their parents' eyes had not had it. But rather bemusement at the pale (mostly) foreigners poking their damp heads everywhere, surprised that so much life existed in a part of the planet they knew so little about. They marveled at the architecture, the vegetation. The paintings—paintings were everywhere—the music, and, of course, the dance.

Do they not dance and paint where they are from? the old women asked each other.

Do they not have tasty food?

Have they no remaining vegetation?

Young and old alike were puzzled. Some were flattered. Most were, for the longest time, wary or indifferent. Few of them remembered the overthrow of their country's monarchy by Europeans in a distant century. Their beautiful country occupied. Their king beheaded, the queen raped. Their country stomped on, drained, for over three hundred years: a time of seeming amnesia, for survival's sake. Few dared to think too closely of the horrors the ancestors endured: of the leaden, pus-colored men on top of them who smelled of stale tobacco, sour sauternes, and rancid cheese. The near nakedness of the Kalimasans drove the sexually repressed Europeans to heights of cruelty as they vainly sought to deny their lust. So much beauty in a world indifferent to their ways, a green and gentle and supple world that was actually repelled by the mountainous thickness of the pale male body in its farty woolen underwear, black cloak, and ugly hat. The people had suffered, in silence, seemingly in a collective sleep. The sleep of shame. Then, as if a cycle had ended, collectively they woke up. They fought back. They became independent, at least in name.

—

She listens to the woman softly snoring beside her, and then, switching off her mind, she begins to stroke her awake. The woman is responsive instantly, as if she'd never really been asleep. She permits my daughter free-roaming access to her heavy breasts, hot to the touch, and to her furry belly from which the scent of sandalwood floats upward through the sheet. My daughter places her nose in the crease of the woman's neck, which, like her breasts, is incredibly warm. The woman rolls over and is suddenly the aggressor, on top of my daughter, straddling her. My daughter has wanted this. She widens her body on the bed and slips off the thin chemise she is wearing in order to permit full contact. The woman flings off her strip of a garment, something barely gathered around her loins, and begins to ride my daughter, hard, as if she would drive her into the mattress that sits on a delicate frame of bamboo.

Her tryst with the Kalimasan boy has left her savage. That, and Susannah's apparent indifference to it. Now she sucks her fiercely, Susannah's breasts full and brown and somehow pleading against Pauline's white teeth and insistent mouth. Between Susannah's breasts sweat flows, which Pauline laps like a dog. Between her legs where Pauline has insinuated her hand there is, already, a stream of wetness. She feels Pauline's fingers, first one, then two, then three, enter her with an authoritative firmness. She is embarrassed to hear herself moan and shamed to hear Pauline's grunt of conquest. Susannah's body starts to move against the woman's hand. Oh, she says. And oh, and oh, and oh. Pauline bites her ears. She laps her body everywhere there is sweat. She keeps her pinned and will not let her rise. When my daughter raises her neck from the bed so that the cords of her neck stand out, Pauline thrusts her long whining tongue into her mouth with such force she pushes Susannah's head almost underneath the pillow. Only her gorged mouth is visible, and Pauline's forehead rests on the pillow that obscures Susannah's face.

Pauline is conscious of the slightest tremor of my daughter's body but she is also venting her "lust" for the Kalimasan boy. She imagines him coming through the bamboo curtain at the foot of the bed, penis—a smooth and heavy one, she is happy to find out—erect, dripping in hope and shy anticipation. She imagines ordering him to the bed, to her backside. Imagines he is in her, driving her, as she drives herself against Susannah, as if she would kill her for distancing from her, slaughter her for her indifference. Bruise her for the days spent indifferent to Pauline, with her head under the covers in bed.

When she retrieves her tongue from my daughter's throat, she laps her armpits, her sides; she claims my daughter's body as she wriggles expertly backward, toward the slippery penis of the boy, whose heat she feels in her cunt, in her ass, in her ovaries and womb. This is not the moment to recall her own grandsons, half the age of the Kalimasan boy. But she does. Sex is like a stew for her, everyone in it at once. She imagines the thrust of the penis of the Kalimasan boy. She feels her own clitoris huge against the body of the woman with whom she is so angry. She wants her grandsons to know this kind of power over a woman, or over a boy. It is the only power over others she wants them to have. The power to give pleasure, ruthlessly, and to leisurely take it.

She is ready to burst. But refuses to do so. She lifts her body off Susannah. Rests on her knees, her hand busy between my daughter's legs. Legs that, though wide, are not wide enough. She pushes them wider. My daughter moans. Feels a wimp. How could she be like this with this woman who so often irritates her? It is a mystery she will not entertain tonight. She feels Pauline's fist, each knuckle distinct, raking her labia, sending heat waves to her womb. She feels fingers and then full warm lips on her breast. But there is a lessening of intensity, a flagging of energy. She peeks through her tangled hair to see what is happening with Pauline. It is as she suspects. Pauline is waiting for her to ask for it. To beg and plead for it. *To thrash against her hand and moan. Oh please, please, go down on me.*

—

This is the moment Pauline loves. In fact, if she thinks about how much she loves it before it happens she will go off and miss what is for her the crowning moment. That moment when all her terrible beauty is acknowledged, her awesome power bowed to, the sensuality of her daring to wear a bathing suit while riding motorcycles driven by Hindu boys in a country run by Muslims, forgiven.

The Kalimasan boy has her breasts now, as she waits, in what seems a royal, even imperial squat, for the plea she knows will come. She has given Susannah deeper orgasms than she has ever known; she feels she controls them. Pauline has the same breasts that she had at thirty. Strong, upright breasts whose slight sag only makes them more supple in the hand. Breasts that have never known a bra. The boy's mouth on her breasts is cool as a melon seed. Waiting for my daughter's surrender she rocks; my daughter's shudder against her clitoris almost sets her off. She moves slightly back from her. It will not do to come now and give up the moment my daughter bares herself.

Please, my daughter says.

Please what? says the woman, stopping the movement of her hand altogether.

My daughter whispers something.

Pauline says, loudly: Speak up!

Lick me, my daughter says, and looks her in the eye.

My daughter hears the sharp intake of the woman's breath. Still looking deep into her eyes, witnessing the lust and the victory, acknowledging it, she reaches up to touch Pauline's clitoris. It is swollen and tremulous, her cunt dripping. Her hand is a dancer in the woman's wet flames. Intoxicated, she raises her hand to her nose. The scent of a woman's sex is like nothing in the world. It is a scent she would crawl for, though Pauline, ever practical, has reminded her it is a scent she already owns.

Pauline pumps her hand slowly up and out of Susannah's body, which grieves its leaving by shivering and shuddering. Every fiber of her body is alert to what is coming to her clit.

—

Pauline would like to make her beg some more. She is in an arrogant, nearly hostile place few of her friends, colleagues, children, and grandchildren ever see. It is powerful there. She loves it. But if she doesn't get on with it, the sight of Susannah, laid out like a feast, will bring her to climax—and she is not ready for that yet. In truth, she can barely believe she has restrained herself for so long, and denied herself the taste of my daughter's core.

Now she is all gentleness, easing her sweaty body between my daughter's legs, ever so gently pressing them wider with the broad width of her own thick shoulders. She flings her lead-colored locks out of her eyes, and slithers down, and sinks.

It is her warm breath my daughter feels. Immediately she is calmed. She settles her body into the bed. Cradles her head exactly in the middle of the pillow. Sighs. *At last.* Touches briefly, gratefully, masterfully, almost negligently, the woman's shoulders and her wild hair. Surrendering, she is all but consumed by her own feelings of power.

Pauline flicks her clitoris with a tongue that seems made of suede, and Susannah begins to moan anew. It is a moan so ani-mallike and guttural, so abandoned and shameless, so full of self-witness, a moan so unlike her day-to-day self, when a certain fastidious haughtiness is often commented on in her character, that it is comical. Leaving passion for just a moment, they both laugh. The bed shakes, as they giggle; a slender bamboo leg cracks. Shit, says Susannah. Pauline raises her head: Next time, she mutters, I'll have you on the floor.

Pauline's mouth captures the whole of Susannah's vulva. There is no little corner of it that at first escapes. It is as if she would suck out the womb and, indeed, she appears to dive for it with her long whining tongue. Only now, at this, the whining tongue sings, and Susannah feels herself mounting to the clouds, and tries to slow herself down from arriving there. Unbidden, in that mo-ment, she thinks of me and of her mother, so often fighting, when she was a child. Only to emerge from our bedroom after a fight completely peaceful, tranquil, with each other. Our every move-ment one of indolence, our every utterance marked by an unfath-omable calm.

MacDoc

Of course Pauline's behavior reminds me of Magdalena's. Of
Maggie. MacDoc.

When Susannah was four, my church sent me as spiritual ad-
visor to Mexico to work among the Mundo Indians. In reality her
mother and I were both anthropologists, but in the early Forties
no one would fund us on any serious expedition. We threw ourselves on the mercy of our church, as black people always do
when all other sources of sustenance fail. We explained what we
had heard about the Mundo: that they were a tiny band of mixed-
race Blacks and Indians who'd fled across the border during the
Civil War; that by now the people, like others of their mixture
near Veracruz, Costa Chica, and elsewhere, thought of themselves not as Africans or as Indians, but as dark-skinned Mexicans. Isolated, however, as they were, they were said to retain
distinct tribal ways that they honored and had never repudiated.
This was mysterious to earlier anthropologists who had attempted to study them, because they were continually being, it
was thought, killed off. They were truly dying out this time,

though, according to the information we had, and it was urgent that we witness their way of life before their demise.

We drove, my wife Langley and I, the entire way, though since the Mundo live in such splendid isolation in the Sierra Madre, where their closest neighbors, the Tarahumara, are still two hundred miles away, we were forced to leave the car at the last hardscrabble mission, its church crumbling, we encountered. The Mundo sent donkeys down for us, and we arrived to find a gathering of friendly, curious villagers preparing barbecued mutton and broiled corn.

Maggie was six. Not a six, however, of innocent cheerfulness. Not a six of languid indolence. Not a six driven merely by the dictates of a playful curiosity. No. She was a six that already stared boldly at anything that interested her. And what interested her, it seemed to me, even at that early age, was men, and what was concealed by their trousers.

My wife did not see this as a problem. Leave the child alone, she advised as we prepared for bed at night, children are curious! I complained that Maggie embarrassed us by her boldness. Her staring and her sidling up to boys three times her age. She is curious, my sweet daughter, said my wife. She laughed. And the young men here *are* magnetic. She shrugged. Come to bed yourself, and don't forget the nightly rubber.

—

Langley made me laugh. Almost each and every night she made me laugh, as she had done the very first night we met; at a society ball thrown by upper-class Blacks for their grown-up Jack and Jill offspring in a sleek and prosperous enclave of Harlem. Her parents had inherited what was referred to at the time, with envy, as "musical money," from a famous uncle who was a jazz composer and performer. After Jack and Jill, which was considered by most black people as a kindergarten for the rich, and after boarding school, she'd gone to college in Maine. I, on the other hand, had worked my way through Hampton Institute in the South, and in fact was so poor that I owned only one suit, the one I was wearing when she asked me to dance.

I was so astonished by this breach of propriety, especially as I noticed her parents looking on, and yet so thrilled by the playful recklessness in her eyes, that I spilled the pink punch I was drinking, all over myself.

You look good in pink, she'd said brusquely, cracking nary a smile and coolly using a dainty, heavenly-scented hanky to dab at my tie. I laughed because it was certainly not what I'd expected her to say.

In Mexico she was a woman split in two. During the day, as the "pastor's" wife, she wore dark colors, even in the midday heat. Or snowy white on feast days, as some of the Indians did. At night she wore nothing at all. Oh, what does God care about what I wear? she had asked the first night we slept together and I was stunned by her beauty, naked, but also profoundly shocked. God gets to wear everything, including us. I suppose I could have forced the issue. But she did not even own a nightgown. Although she did find something, and hold it up. It looked serviceable and was the color of poached salmon, "flesh colored," it claimed on the label. There were stays. Shall I sleep in this slip your mother gave me? she asked. Frowning, draping the ugly color against her peachy skin.

—

Susannah was fascinated by the gigantic pots that the women made in heaps. Some were so big she could put her whole head inside. The Mundo women used only three colors: the red of earth, which was the pot itself and came from the local clay; the black of charcoal; and the white of lime, used as decoration, which after baking in the fire was not white but gray. There were few designs on Mundo pots: their beauty was in the burnished smoothness, the rich symmetry of their form. Their usefulness. The rough, un-polished pots which they also made were bound with strips of goatskin; these were filled with grain and strapped to the backs of donkeys that took them down to the market for sale.

We were there when the railroad came within a day's journey of their mountainous territory, almost a century after it was begun in Mexico; and there to see the beginning of the end of the long line of donkeys snaking down the mountain in the blinding sun.

—

Langley studied pottery making with the women. She learned to dig the clay, clean it, wedge it, roll the long coils that formed the sides of each pot, and then to kneel before the growing pot as it magically rose from her shallow grass basket, her tongue often poking out the corner of her mouth in rapt concentration, as the other women's did. There was in building a pot a distinct feeling of prayer, she said. Especially in the first, beginner's lessons, when she did pray that her slippery, wobbly construction would not slump to the ground. Of course, she said, from watching their mothers make pots, primitive man would assume God made men from clay. Though why, seeing their mothers' work, they'd think God male, she could not grasp.

—

From the window of my study in the small house we were given I watched them. Susannah and her mother intent on learning a skill. Enthralled by the women's serene mastery of their life-sustaining craft. For it was in their pots that the tribe's food and drink were stored. And Maggie, off in the arroyos with the wild Indian boys who were already teaching her such feminine skills as how to leap from one formidable boulder to another without breaking a leg. And to run, as they did, like the wind.

I did not understand her spirit. I yearned for guidance. It seemed to be necessary to tame her, though no one among the Indians or in my own family showed any signs of thinking so. The Indians, I think, admired her. By the age of ten she was like, and even resembled, one of their sons. Their own daughters, however, were, like Susannah, demure, interested in women's things. There was not one as wild as MacDoc, as Maggie by now was called. She had wanted to be known as Mad Dog, but I drew the line there.

MacDoc. My daughter MacDoc. At puberty I began to keep her from her friends, the wild boys who were now, some of them, beginning to notice her femaleness, and to attempt to protect her. They did not think she should jump over boulders as recklessly as before, or run about the village with quite the same abandon. Magdalena flaunted a transformation they could not match. Did they have buds forming on their chests like hers? No! Did they have hair beginning to grow on their lower bodies, as she did? No! Well then, they were still children. And not women. Only green little boys!

She would weep and rage over her homework in the room she shared with Susannah. When the wild boys came to look for her, a hurt puzzlement in their eyes, I sent them away. I insisted that she be called Magdalena.

This was one of the reasons Langley and I fought. She did not agree that Magdalena did anything wrong in expressing her own nature.

But what if she gets pregnant? I said. Imagining the expense of supplying rubbers to every young man in the village.

My wife was quiet. My thinking this way about our daughter disappointed her. It was one of those silences I'd come to read. It meant: Really, why am I with you? Finally she said: But it does not seem to me that Mad Dog wishes to sleep with anyone, other than with her sister.

This was so like Langley. To be blind to the obvious and to be subversive about it too.

Magdalena, I said.

Oh, sure, she said. Don't you understand there is no more Magdalena? There is no Maggie either. Both Magdalena and Maggie are finished.

But that is what we named her, I said.

Yes, said Langley, and obviously before we knew who she was.

Well, she cannot be called Mad Dog, I said. She is the daughter of a minister!

But mad dogs here are considered wise, said my wife. Perhaps you should not have brought us here. She sighed, and took my hand.

You must talk to Mad Dog, she said, and explain to her why she cannot be both Mad Dog and your sane daughter.

—

I tried.

By now Maggie, Magdalena, Mad Dog, MacDoc was fifteen. And taller than I. Except for summers, which she and Susannah often spent with their grandparents on Long Island, she had grown up in the Sierra Madre. She was a silent, brooding young woman whose pleasure lay, almost exclusively, in reading. I liked this. Not the silence, or the brooding, but the calm. Reading at her desk or under a tree or in the shade of a boulder in the yard, she seemed, especially from a distance, quite ladylike, demure. Because she was less active she began to gain weight, and to acquire a lumbering tilt to her gait; a condition that worried Langley but did not particularly bother me.

—

She eats so much more than usual. Haven't you noticed? asked my wife.

In an attempt to show affection I would sometimes heap more food on her plate.

I monitored her wardrobe. Her dresses were long. Her necklines high.

Soon you will be sixteen, I said. And a woman. At that time you may choose a new name. I glanced sidelong at her. Where we walked, because it was spring, coming into summer, our path was carpeted with tiny blue flowers that popped open after each rain. Before us the mountains rose in a hazy mauve and shaggy blue-gray splendor. I remarked to myself that she had lived in this gorgeousness practically her entire life. The impact of such beauty on her soul would have to be tremendous, I mused, and was likely to be a ballast for her throughout the wild storms of life.

I know we are going home soon, she said. Is that why I get to choose a new name?

It was, really. And I said so. On Long Island, in Sag Harbor, you will need a name others can relate to. Your cousins, for instance. She frowned. She disliked her cousins, who were dressed exactly like dolls, and sat and stared out unblinking, also like dolls. She had always longed to put dirt on their dresses. And probably had.

I shall be called June, she said.

I was surprised. It wasn't the name of a person but of a month. Still it was feminine, soft. She might have done worse.

And if you object, she continued, I shall be called July.

Oh no, I said, laughing, attempting to squeeze her shoulders as she swerved away from me. It is perfect. And that is the month we are in!

Yes, she said drily, without returning my gaze.

—

I don't think we know we have lost our daughters until they are gone. But perhaps I should, in modesty, speak only for myself. When we came down from the walk in the mountains it is true that I felt I missed, was missing, something. I felt a vacancy around my heart, an emptiness. The conquest had been easy. Too easy. I knew she must have planned and plotted to escape the corral of a new name but in the end, without struggle, she had given in. What did it mean? And why didn't I care?

We all began to call her June. It is without question a beautiful name. Elegant. Evocative of mystery. Warmth. It is promise itself. It says many things—all about the moisture, readiness, richness of summer. June is always the new beginning of whatever is bountiful. I said some of this to her. I mentioned the illustrious people, poets and musicians, painters, who carried the name. By now my daughter only smiled when I spoke, never showing her sharp white teeth. I felt she tolerated rather than engaged me. As we packed to leave the mountains for good she hummed a pagan song. Something about the oneness of the unclothed human body and the nakedness of the sky. *Por la luz, por la luz . . . by the light, by the light,* seemed a melancholy refrain.

It was a song not permitted in our church. The small white chapel, the inside of which startled visitors with its vivid blue and green and yellow murals. Its starry sky overhead. Its fields of corn with rows marching into each window. Its big green watermelons painted, with red insides dripping and black seeds painted like eyes, just above the pulpit. No one ever took credit or responsibility for painting the inside of the church, which was as different from the outside as night from day. Yet the paintings were never permitted to fade. When my superiors from Long Island came to see the state of my mission they were dismayed by it. Heathens, they sniffed. I was not disturbed. It reminded me of the summers I had spent in North Carolina with my grandparents who farmed. The lushness of corn fields there, the dark, starry sky at night, the immense transcendent beauty and taste of my grandfather's watermelons. The murals inside the church made me less lonesome, as I fought the blasphemous, unbidden thought that the appreciation of corn and melon is more universal than the appreciation of Christ.

Some of their songs were permitted in church. And many standard hymns—"Onward, Christian Soldiers," for instance—were translated into their language. This seemed only right, since we were in their territory. But not the song June sang, with its carnal message of unity with creation and no credit to a Creator. I had heard it only once before, the month we'd arrived, ten years ago. It was a chant, really, repetitious and monotonous as all chants are. The tribe had seemed hypnotized by it. Taken someplace deeper than church, where they had to stay riveted on the convoluted ideas, customs, and lives of foreigners in a book, the Bible, that had no particular fascination for them. The song was not written down. How had she learned it? What did it signify? Were the people still chanting this song in secret ceremonies? June obviously knew. And knew as well that I did not know. This was her power, exposed. It was a power, not only over the God we'd come to share with these people, it was a power over me.

Twigs

I did not know until much later that Susannah was outside our bedroom door while Daddy was punishing me. It must have been as incomprehensible to her as it was to me. I knew I had disobeyed him, but he was after all a minister, or at least putting up a mighty show of being one. He'd even gradually graduated from pastor, wearing a plain tan colored suit on Sundays, to priest, and wore black every day. His profession, as he explained it to me and Susannah, was based on the forgiveness of other people's sins. In the long white dresses he ordered for me and the Mary Jane shoes, the quaint colorful shawls he purchased from the village weavers, I'm sure he thought me hobbled. But he did not understand my passion for riding horses, or my particular passion for riding Vado, the black stallion that belonged to Manuelito. And so, of course, he did not know where to look when it was clear I had escaped the nest. That from the look of things I had escaped at will, even while the door was locked. That even Susannah, his adoring flunky, had been in cahoots with me, and had lied to him. Oh, Daddy dear, as she sweetly and sickeningly called him, our

Magdalena is sleeping. Oh, Daddy dear, our Magdalena is in the water closet. Oh, Daddy dear, she seems to have fainted from stomach cramps.

But on that last day I did not sneak. Manuelito and Vado appeared on a rise I could see from my window, and while the family ate lunch, I went out to them. I hitched my long skirt high up on my thighs and Manuelito swung down for me. We were equally brown, equally bold of dark and reckless eye. We'd been twin spirits since the day I arrived with my family so many years ago. And Manuelito had pinched me in the ribs while Daddy led his first froggy-throated prayer, a prayer he'd learned in the car on the way down and obviously didn't believe, and I'd promptly stepped on his bare foot—in my leather-soled North American shoes—hard.

It was like that with us. No tears, lots of pain. We did not speak of loving each other. No. That was not our way at all. We instead discovered bird's nests together, abandoned trails, poisoned wells, vulture feasts, rattlesnake beds, a valley of bluebells early in the spring. All these we shared almost wordlessly. And when we touched each other there was a casual ownership about it, an ownership that claimed just the moment of the actual touching, nothing more. But what this meant was that when Manuelito touched just one curl of my wayward hair—for in Mexico we were not bothered to straighten it—that one seemingly absentminded fingering was felt as something alive, curling, electric, as far down as my toes.

The place we went to was familiar. In fact, it was our home. We went home. We went to our house. I love to think of it this way even now. It was a shallow cave in the side of the mountains. A rusty shrub obscured our door. But from inside you could see through the shrub, and then our living room faced a valley. And it was in our yard that, in springtime, the wild bluebells grew.

We furnished our home with just a blanket, hidden behind some rocks, and a water jug, refilled from Manuelito's goatskin each time we came. In our home, I was called by my name, Magdalena. It was only in Manuelito's voice that it sounded right. He said it softly. With such respect! He said he liked the sound of it especially whispered, like a prayer, against my clitoris. When his mouth formed my name there, and I experienced the feathery movement of his breath, I felt my whole self seen. Everything in me, including everything in my soul, seemed to run into his arms. Manuelito, my love, my *angelito*, my pretty, pretty boy, I whispered back to him. And the light and the mountains and the bluebells . . . all of it was us.

I thought I could have become pregnant since I was fourteen, for that was the first time I lay down with Manuelito, himself one year my junior. But when I told him this later, he laughed and said no, that for one whole year we had fumbled blindly, for he had not known quite what to do. Everything we did pleased me, and I was fulfilled simply to lie close beside him and nibble at the corners of his mouth, or lick his eyelids. His lashes were so long that, when he closed his eyes, they appeared to be small black fans.

Maybe by fifteen years of age I might have embarrassed my father by carrying Manuelito's child. But by then his father and uncles and older brothers had taught him what all the young boys were taught during initiation: how not to impregnate anyone. I was safe. Worshipped is how it felt. To know myself so thought of, so cared about, to know that he would withdraw from me at just the right moment, no matter that I held him tight. To feel in myself and in my response to Manuelito such depths of trust and desire caused me to feel innately holy, as if our love made a magic circle about me that cloaked me in a private invisibility when I was obliged to return home.

Manuelito's soft tongue on my nipples, his soft words in my ear, his sturdy penis moving inside me. The beauty of his brown body above me, warming the shaded, sometimes quite chilly cave. The light that was drawn around the shrub guardian to suffuse our space. All these images I stored up for the time, later, when I would be in the North. A brown girl whose father was a minister and who had had the unusual experience of living years of her life in the faraway mountains of Mexico.

This time my father knew. I wonder if he'd known other times as well. For there was a craftiness, a streak of crafty meanness, in him. Perhaps he deliberately waited until we were about to leave the mountains before confronting me. Manuelito had given me a silver belt—rather, it was a leather belt that was covered with small silver disks. He'd made it himself. I kept it in bed with me, underneath my pillow. It was with this that my father punished me.

This is not an unusual story. I know that now. Fathers attack their children around the world, every day. But I did not know this then. I knew I was wild. Disobedient. Wayward and headstrong. But I did not understand his violence, after I had just experienced so much pleasure. So much sweetness. If he had known, if I could have told him, I felt he should have been happy for me. If in fact he loved me, as he often said he did. But no, he thrashed me in silence. I withstood it, in silence. I sent my spirit flying out the window to land on the glistening black back of Vado, my arms circling Manuelito's neat waist. We flew along our favorite trail through the mountains, bluebells vibrant at our feet. Apparently Susannah sobbed for both of us. On her knees outside our bedroom, her eye to the keyhole; my mother behind her, packing with an air of righteous resignation. Once again, because of his stubborn behavior, she said, she was going to leave my father.

She never did.

After the beating she was warm to me and cool to him for several weeks. Then, it simply evened out again. The temperature in our house—the roomy, boxy one with the lawn, in Sag Harbor—became normal. He moved, finally, into the big bedroom where she slept alone at night. Sounds came from that room, voices, late into the night. Within a month, or less, my father loved my mother back to himself.

But something had happened to precious little Susannah at the keyhole. It was as if she'd peered into our simple, girlish bedroom through the keyhole and witnessed her gentle, compassionate father turn into Godzilla. She would never be loved back to her daddy again. With time, as I understood how severely the twig was bent in that moment of her horror and disbelief, my revenge against my father, a revenge so subtle Susannah would not realize its damage to her for another thirty years, was born. As for my father, he would never again be permitted to really know or enjoy his favorite little tree.

Twins

Susannah is writing a novel that explores the relationship she had with a man after her marriage to the Greek. But she is having difficulties. She cannot write in any sex. *Write it in,* I screech from the celestial sidelines. *Put the sex right on up in there!* Even if it's nothing but the copulating dogs you saw from your window as a five-year-old when we lived in Mexico: you thought they were twins, that being hooked together in that way was what being twins meant. Your mother and I laughed, and I remember thinking that even your little mind was cute. Or think of the giraffes you saw doing it years later in Africa, their long necks like chimneys. You stared, and started to fan yourself. Your lover smiled to himself. That night he shocked and stirred you, when he entered you from behind. It is not so big a deal! I want her to know. As I see her, crippled in a place that should be free, and still, after all these years, perplexed by the memory of her sister's stubborn face and the sound of the whistling silver belt. And my own face, what did she read there, what message about the consequences of a searing passion, ecstatic sex?

Ritual

If a man has not committed too grave a crime it is not impossible to love himself back into his wife's arms. It is even easy to do this, if she is sick, weary, or weak in some way. Langley, when we left the mountains, was all of these things. My behavior with our daughters exasperated her. My assumption that Susannah was pure and Magdalena a tramp. She had left the home and social circle that she knew in Long Island to follow our shared anthropological star to Mexico. There she had dutifully masqueraded as a pastor's wife. And even gaily lived in sin, after I elevated myself to priest. She had, being Langley, gone beyond this role to become a sunny and welcomed force among the village women, making friends she cherished and busily writing down every aspect of their ways.

Her sacrifice was in the isolation she endured, far from her family and friends; the absence of a daily newspaper, the *Times*; the remoteness of our splendid wilderness in the thin air that we loved.

My own remorse for having struck the child was great. In the solitude of my ostracism, an estrangement from all my girls,

Langley as well as June and Susannah, I contemplated my error. I could find no justification for it. Yes, the child was willful, disobedient. She was born that way. The idea that a child comes into the world a clean slate is a ridiculous one. When she was two and we tried out the notion of shoes on her feet, she rebelled. At five she said a final no, thank you, to oatmeal. At six she wanted a zipper at the front of her pants just like I had. And then the red zippered pants Langley had found for her caused offense. In her child's mind—but after how many previous lifetimes as a discriminating being! my friends the Mundo shamans might say—they did not seem serious enough. After all, I never wore red trousers.

I prayed over it. Spare the rod, spoil the child. One says that and swallows down one's immediate protest. Stifles the voice that hates the rod. Would never, on its own, have even thought about the rod. There was something in me, I found, that followed ideas, beliefs, edicts, that had been put into practice, into motion, before I was born. And this "something" was like an internalized voice, a voice that drowned out my own. Beside which, indeed, my own voice began to seem feeble. Submissive. And when I allowed myself to think about that submission I thought of myself as having been spiritually neutered. And thought, as well, of the way Langley, Magdalena, and even the all-accepting Susannah sometimes looked at me. In dismay and disappointment. Daddy, the girls seemed to ask, where is your own spark? Langley seemed resigned to the fact that it was missing.

How long it took me to realize it was the *me*ness of me that was missing! That next to the men of the Mundo village, even before we could comfortably converse with them, I was a shadow. It wasn't, as I used to think, that I wore the long black coat and black hat and trousers that marked my occupation as shepherd of souls, no. In some odd way I was, the self of me, canceled out. I was a man mouthing words that sparkled, but going through the motions of my own life.

Except, in our most private life, with Langley. There was grounding in her presence. In her arms. Grounding especially in her laughter, the naked shedding of roles that was her sleep. I loved even to hear her snore, though to awaken and see me peering at her as she did so embarrassed her. Then she would grab a pillow and jam it over her head. And I would tug it off, and tussle with her. Her warm naked body the fire of life. Her breath the breathing of life. And when she was sick and weary and weak, and when she cried in frustration or when she was angry enough at me to throw chairs—then it seemed to me I loved her so much I was in danger of forgetting the voice inside my head, forgetting even the voice I began to recognize as "God's."

We had agreed, even before we were married, that we would never lay a hand on our child. We believed in correction, which we thought could be accomplished by reason and consistency; we did not believe in corporal punishment. This had been of such importance to us that we had discussed it thoroughly, over years, until Langley felt it was safe for her to bear a child. By beating her eldest daughter, to the point of actually drawing blood, caused by the disks on the accursed belt I used, I had betrayed her completely.

We were beaten in slavery! she screamed, weeping as if her heart would break.

She cried every night and would not let me enter the big bedroom with the gauze curtains that blew limply in the muggy summer heat. And each night, as soon as the girls were asleep, I made my way there, to her door. On my knees, outside the locked door, I pleaded.

Only forgive me, I said. I do not expect, or deserve, anything more.

Please do not cry, I said. Crying now, myself. I am not worth one tear that falls from your beautiful eyes.

Don't break any more of your precious treasures, I said. As a crystal vase we'd kept in storage while in Mexico—a vase she loved—crashed against the door.

Everything in me wanted to break down the door, pin her flailing arms to her sides, drag her to the bed, lick away every tear, drink from her flowing body, and pour my whole being into hers. But I, my heart breaking, could not rise from my knees. She had seen me turn into a monster; how could I ever expect her to forget? I fell asleep there, growing cramped and chilled as the night wore on.

In the morning, her face wrinkled as a crone's and tear-stained, she opened the door, sniffed at me as if I were disagreeable garbage, and stepped gingerly around my cold, ashen, and yellowing feet.

—

This nightly ritual seemed to go on forever. During the day I called June June. I took her and Susannah to the YWCA, where they swam and made macramé wall hangings. I took them shopping. I went to Montauk with them, where an old friend of mine had the very last house before the Island petered out into the sea. In the nonexistent traffic there, I taught June to drive.

Preoccupied, I tried to imagine my life without Langley. I could not. For without Langley all of it was just going through the motions, following the dictate of the voice in my ear, the emptiness in my soul. But there was no warmth without her, no fire. No rebellion of my own angel to enjoy. No surprise.

She became so weak from her grief that when she stepped over me in the mornings, she stumbled. She was eating next to nothing. I was the same. I think we both had fevers, for our nightly exertions took their toll.

I begged her to let me take care of her. She laughed, a mean laugh. And tossed her hair, which since our return from Mexico she'd both straightened and bobbed. In her plum-colored silk pajamas and fluffy-toed mules she was a different woman—which I found amazing and almost unbearably exciting. She had also begun taking courses in comparative anthropology at the local college. It drove me crazy not to be making love to her and, while loving her, learning her new thoughts.

I decided to learn golf.

It did not work. I disliked the cap. The cart. The balls. And hadn't I heard somewhere that the green itself, because of the chemicals used to keep it so, was toxic?

One morning she did not leave her room. By then I had dragged my mattress from my room and slept on it just beside her door. After half an hour of waiting, I went inside. Surprised to find that the door was not locked. She could not get out of bed. Seeing this, I felt—it is almost impossible to describe, except to say I felt the mother in me fully ripen and rise to the occasion. Suddenly I was all over the room at once, tending to Langley; changing the sheets, opening the windows, adjusting the curtains, picking up newspapers and books from the floor. Then, down in the kitchen, I made soup, squeezed oranges, made toast. Got the children out of the house. Then I came back, watched Langley eat, tucked her in, and went to my room to dress.

During the day I looked in on her. Fed her. Went to the market for anything she said she had a hankering for—the father in me loving the activity of sallying forth! And in the evening I dragged out all the records we'd stored in her parents' basement before we went to Mexico, the records to which we'd danced before the voice in my head got the better of me, and I lit a candle, only one because it was so hot, and Langley had by now reverted to the woman I knew. The heat had made her hair go back to its naughty kinkiness, and perspiration had ruined the silk pajamas, and she didn't know where the mules were, and she loved being naked anyhow.

And now I waited. I was waiting to see in Langley's brown eyes, which sometimes looked maroon, if she still wanted me, old man, sinner, beast, creature that I was. If she remembered how it felt to be with me. To be pinned to the bed by me. To be herself riding me. Did she think of the taste of me, which she said she loved, or remember the feeling of me tasting her, my tongue eager and intent as a spaniel's? Or did she remember how hot nights made loving even better because bodies stuck together? And there was more noise and slipperiness and more moisture of all kinds to absorb. And did she remember my telling her, when we made love, and she gave herself completely to me, *Baby I love you and Baby I love you is the most erotic thing I know?*

Naked, nappy, bright-eyed, and almost well, she began to study me. I felt it immediately. She did it when my back was turned. On my way to the kitchen. Out the door to the store. Bending to retrieve the spoon she'd dropped. The one she'd licked long and suggestively with her rapidly recovering tongue.

She caught me watching, and laughed. You have a tongue fetish, she said.

Grace

To love someone over many years is all the opportunity you need to learn how to love them back from anywhere.

A death in the family? A wonderful chance! Or so it was with us, and with the death of her little brother, Jocko. Why he was called Jocko no one seemed to know, for he was no sportsman. As a child he adopted the persona of Zorro, the mysterious masked man of the Mexican West. According to Langley, he sewed himself a cape and a mask and wore as well a large black hat pulled low over his nearly obscured eyes. He carried a lariat. He rode a fabulous horse, which he constructed out of the sound of pounding hooves.

So there he'd come, Langley said, prancing and neighing.

And did he run into things? I asked.

Never, she said. His horse was well trained. And he kept this up until, nearly, he went away to boarding school. She paused. I wonder who he became there.

Yes, I said. Who would Zorro turn into at boarding school?

And, she added thoughtfully, how would he stifle the sounds of his horse?

Once Jocko came to see us in the mountains. He was tall and thin, with close-cropped hair and a beautiful nose. He smiled easily and often, as if at an inner pleasure. He was vague, however, about his life. All he told us was that he worked "behind the scenes" in Hollywood. Doing stunts, doing hair. Doing whatever. He drove a stylish car, black and shining, and favored black clothing. Except for a pair of silver boots.

At his funeral Langley wept and held my hand tightly. She had memories that she said suddenly rose around her in the church: memories of being the prized damsel in distress whom Zorro saved and saved. And though he never offered to marry her, as her other brother, who played Tom Mix, often did, he offered friendship, which she imagined—because he offered it and was so dashing in his cape—a much more lasting and final thing.

Of course, she whispered tearfully, with the trace of a Southern accent that crept into her voice whenever she felt sad, in order to rescue me he had to first place me in distress. Here she wept copiously. Sniffling loudly, she continued. How many times he left me bound and gagged somewhere nobody would even think to look! God, it's a wonder I'm not the one who's dead.

Funerals are an opportunity to grow steadily more capable in one's protector role. The shoulder to lean on, the ear to whisper into. The calming hand to hold. They are the opportunity to be still and stoic and present for your woman. Responsive to her sighs and moans. And it is not as far as one would think from the gravesite to the bed.

Jocko left only ashes to be buried, and to Langley he left the silver boots, which fit her perfectly. Inside one of them he'd left a note: Fantasy was the reality of my life. Thank you for enjoying it with me. Of course, wearing the boots, reading the note, tromping about the bedroom feeling the boots on her feet and holding the note in her hand, with me helping her to a glass of wine, turning on the electric fan, and helping her to undress, soon Langley stood before me in her slip.

Tears had made her eyes red. Wiping her nose so much had made it larger; her nostrils flared. Her carefully coifed hair now sprang up and out from her head like a spiky rose. There was the realization, as well, that her powder was all streaked. She'd chewed off her lipstick. She didn't smell, in the heat, as fresh as when she'd left home.

Oh, her favorite brother had died and left her! Tromp of boots. Gulp of white wine. Take the roses away, she cannot bear to see them. Where are her bath salts? Oh, she is a wreck. A hag. Look at that run in her stocking! Oh, death. She'll soon be dead herself!

But, lucky for me, I am there to witness this trauma, as well I should be. I am there to say, Oh, it is only a little run. And I'll put the roses outside the door, and your bath salts are just where they always are, beside the tub. And I will run a bath for you. And here is a dish of black figs, I know how you love them. And can I pour you a little more wine?

And by now I am completely seduced by the sight of my bedraggled, nearly naked woman, the slip by now wriggled and coaxed down to her knees. And then by my completely naked woman, who, naked, reaches once more for the silver boots, which she'd kicked off in a fit of despair. Puts them on. Looks at herself, looks at me in the mirror across from the bed, looks at the bed. Me. Herself naked in the silver boots.

I am still fully clothed. I know how fine I look in my suit. Through it all I have not even unloosened (as they say down South) my tie. I know this woman well. To be buck naked while I'm sharply dressed makes her wetter than lying in a fish pond. By now, she will be hot to the touch, sweaty. If she comes up to me, twines herself about me, rubs herself against my leg, she will slime me. I shiver at the thought.

After many years together you learn how to wait. You want the slime to be there. So that when you touch her there you feel as if the sun is shining in your loins.

What is your name today? she says, coming up to me and studying me carefully.

Today my name is . . . I say, looking into her eyes, feeling the sun raising me up, with only a small fear of saying the wrong thing . . . my name is *husband*.

For just a moment she is completely still. I elaborate: I am Langley's very lucky husband. I am the man taking care of her. She smiles and moves into my arms, laying her head on my chest. Don't worry, that is the correct answer, she says softly, exhaling a ragged breath. And my heart breaks around her, oceanic and warm as a kiss.

I begin very slowly to caress the back of her head, where the naps fairly snap around my fingers. I ease my fingers down the furrow of her back, into the crevice of her backside. I clutch her to me.

Jocko is gone, she murmurs.

I kiss her mouth, lightly, a child's kiss, when she says this. Her bushwoman's nose. My hands by now cradle her bushwoman's butt. I linger a long time in her neck. I rub her ears with my own.

Suddenly, she sniffs. Pulls back. I need a bath, I think, she says. Testing the waters. Okay, I say, not moving. Not letting go of her. She understands. Sighs. Relaxes. Bending, I inhale her, my penis by now an eager puppy against her legs. Over her sloping breasts and erect black nipples I roam, in total time suspension; and when I dip my fingers into the place where life begins I stagger from the wetness of life I have found. I love the scent so much I wrap my whole hand in it and smear it on my hair.

At this, as if stricken in her womb, and literally frowning with desire, she takes my flushed face between her hands and pulls my head to hers. She opens her mouth and sticks her tongue between my teeth. Pressing hard, without pity. Until I nearly lose my breath. She kisses me so hard and for so long I fall backward on the bed, my knees weak. With one hand she cradles the back of my neck, with the other she seems to flick my clothes away. And when she sees how I have risen she promptly sits on me and fucks me, crying. This is for Jocko, she says, with mournful intensity. Still wearing the silver boots, she kicks the sheet away.

Later, restored, she came merrily back to the bed in which she'd left me. A jug of orange juice under one arm, toast and fried eggs on a blue plate in one hand. As we wolfed down the food— she was on her way to class—she told me about the blue wisteria that was blooming for a second time, just where it left its trellis and arched over our door. She had thought wisteria bloomed only once a year; and now this one was blooming twice. Just after her brother's death. She blinked a smile at Jocko. Chewed her egg.

And had I really been fucked so hard I intended to stay in bed forever?

Grinning, she kissed me on the forehead, grimaced at the smell of my hair, and dusted toast crumbs from my chin. Commented on the good fortune we enjoyed in my being someone who only needed to work on Sundays, and then headed, her body fluid as grace, to the door.

Nothing's wrong with Daddy, I heard her, through a fog, tell the girls two days later. He's in bed, reading the Bible.

Inches

By the time I really looked at the girls again, it seemed they had grown inches in all directions. As though harking back to some unknown ancestral Amazon, both girls were tall enough now to look down on both our heads. It was an unexpected state of affairs that at times puzzled and unnerved me. June especially seemed to take perverse pleasue in gobbling food and, over my protest, being able to hold whatever she was enjoying well above my reach.

Twenty Kisses

The Greek is wondering what happened to his marriage. He wonders it because he can hear Whitney Houston singing. She is
promising to love someone always. Yes, but not that guy, Susannah had said. He is on a boat in the Ionian Sea near the island of
Skidiza, where he was born. The sea is, as the brochures say, im-
possibly blue. Although today it looks green. In a certain light it is
turquoise. He remembers my daughter for the oddest reasons.
One is that she taught him so much about himself; his history,
culture, heritage. Taught him to look at it, in fact. He'd thought
it something to dump. To shed like excess baggage in the New
World. He'd get ready to heave something overboard—brocaded
pillowcases with tassels handmade by a remote grandma, or a
faded, tarnished, bent silver spoon he'd eaten from as a baby, and
she'd say: No, wait. Let me feel it. Let me have a look at it. He
had a trunk of old junk from when he was a boy. Even the trunk
looked grotesque in America. Heavy, wooden, obviously made by
a clumsy hand. She saw its beauty. To keep him from throwing it
out, she bought it from him. Paid a dollar and twenty kisses.
Kisses carefully doled out after any disagreement, any quarrel.

It was she who said the Ancients. Who? he'd asked. And she had laughed, tugging a handful of his wiry locks. The Ancients had no word for blue—which made them stupid, in his opinion—and so they described the Aegean and perhaps the Ionian too as being maroon. Purple. Red, like dark blood.

And so he thought of her, as the boat headed into the sunset and the water turned to wine, and as he rubbed oil into the back of the starlet he'd pursued since spotting her slinging tofu burgers in a restaurant in Brentwood, on the very far side of North America.

Susannah had longed to visit Greece, and Skidiza. They'd left New York on a Friday and arrived in his village on Sunday, just as his parents were coming home from church. It was as if they'd changed worlds.

He was self-conscious about the backwardness of his parents' home. The gullies in the road leading up to it, the dust in the courtyard, the cracked mud of its whitewashed walls. The humanlike bellowing of the goats, the bray of the ancient (a true Ancient, he joked) donkey. His father's rough hands, his mother's fat. Susannah did not seem to notice any of these things, but commented instead on the warmth of his mother's smile, his father's tender embrace of his long-wandering son. The way the white walls complemented the golden grass, the rows of olive trees.

The food was delicious, as it had always been. Grilled lamb. A salad of tomatoes, garlic, cucumbers, olives. The fresh bread melted in their mouths. Petros translated for them. They wanted to know Susannah's age. A woman in her forties, and looking so young! That was America! Her family background. Whether she had siblings. Whether they all lived. What were the diseases that took the lives of babies in America? Petros was surprised to hear this question from his mother. She went on to tell Susannah, who leaned forward in her chair to touch his mother's hands, that three of her own children died shortly after birth. Of a chill or of a sweat or of a cough that would not go away. His mother wiped her eyes as she recalled their deaths. His father looked sad, and exhibited as well an air of helplessness, as if the losses had occurred only yesterday. No one had told Petros of his lost siblings, or if they had he had not registered a meaning. Now his mother looked tenderly at him, a look that felt as if she were cuddling him with her eyes. Petros, and his brother Anand, who always wants to be looking after people and who should have been a priest, are all God has left to us, she said, bowing her head slightly and crossing herself.

He was grateful to Susannah for drawing them out—two dour old Greeks dressed in black (as he assumed they must look to her, an American); he cherished her for being present, receptive. He could not quite believe his good fortune: to have gone to America poor, and to have found a well-educated, middle-class wife who loved Greece and was genuine. It did not seem, Susannah's interest in his parents, in his culture, American. No, he thought of coolness when he thought of America, the real America. He definitely thought of blue eyes. And yet, here he sat with his brown-skinned wife, her big brown eyes as expressive as his own. The puzzle of his attraction to her, who might have been a darker sister, a slight exasperation to him.

There was a day, perhaps it was even the evening of the day of their arrival: out in the courtyard that was slowly cooling from the day's heat, the sunflowers nodding in the corners like drowsy old men. They sat around a wooden table, the very one into whose sides he'd carved his and Anand's names while they were boys, the day that Anand had vowed never to abandon Greece and he had vowed to leave it as soon as he could, and Susannah, her eyes watering, drank ouzo for the first time, and nibbled a home-preserved olive. Look! she whispered urgently to him. Look at this! She was looking down and pointing at the table. Was he to look at the brown loaves of bread, with their soft white ends; or at the dark olives in an old blue crockery dish he remembered from when he was a boy? Did she mean the two dusty green bottles of wine? The fava beans swimming in oil? Did she mean, Look at the peaches—which did, in fact, smell exactly of heaven? Did she mean, Regard the plums, luscious and dark as goddesses? But no; she meant, giving it a tug, Look at the tablecloth!

The oilcloth with a black background and cabbage roses of white, red, and pink on which all the delicious food lay. Remember this, she whispered. This tablecloth. *It is a sign.* Then, laughing, she made the motion of zippering her lips—a movement, a signal for secrecy they shared—that made them cackle loudly, as the ouzo hit the bottom of their jet-lagged bellies, and the old ones looked on in amusement and a little alarm.

It was the beginning of the end, even so. Even though, that very night, in the small white bedroom next to his parents' room, the room that had been his as a boy, they, with their firmly zippered lips, moved as silently against each other as two snakes. Kissing was not speaking and was therefore exempt from the ban. Slipping to the floor, at the foot of the bed, silently thanking her for loving his parents and not considering them grotesque, as he had feared, he took her small brown foot into his large pale hand and kissed its sole. Sitting on the floor beside the bed, tired, a bit drunk, he made not a sound as he brushed both her feet, back and forth and back and forth, with his thick mustache. The bed shook with her laughter, but she also did not make a sound. She felt herself warm, beginning to tingle inside, and thought: All play leads up to this moment.

Through the wall they heard the old ones shifting their bodies. They heard them sigh, begin to snore. By then he had climbed up into the bed, was on top of her, was inside her, was soaking in her scent of lemongrass and cloves. He floated on her, his penis a rod, a branch of the olive tree, no, the very olive tree itself, whose olives she loved. The ancestral tree that fed all of Greece. Moving in her, to his parents' snores.

Long and sweetly they played, connecting worlds that rarely glimpsed each other, and then usually in travel brochures; continents foreign to each other as the moon. More foreign, because the moon at least could be seen. Cultures connected only by the warmth of a mother's eye, a new daughter's receptive look. A lover's kiss. He could feel her orgasm coming. It was a shivering, like wind, around his tree. And as it blew downward he raised his trunk to greet it, his free mouth—with its wild mustache like a wreath of leaves—in silence growing wider and fuller over her own.

He had thought she might become pregnant from that night. He had had the distinct impression of their being in the embrace of nature. Certainly he felt as if he had planted something in my daughter that would not cease to grow. Exactly where she was broken, in her willing response to him, to his parents' sweetness, the delicious food and burning drink, to the balding, fading oil-cloth on the table, to the little white room itself, he was not able to discern. And yet she had turned from him, finally, that sacred night, and had fallen asleep. Satiated. But incomprehensibly empty.

The Reason You
Fell in Love

She was curious. A woman of curiosity. That was so American of her. She wondered why many of the old women wore black. Why they stepped aside with deference when men passed. What was that quality of resignation in their joy?

She noticed that the leader of our country had a tall blonde from the American Midwest as his wife. And that all the little wifelets of his deputies had lightened their own dark hair by several shades. She asked me about the killing of the adulterous woman in *Zorba the Greek*. Did Kazantzakis tell the truth? And if he did, did such things still happen?

As she forged ahead, I saw a shift occur in my mother's look. Very odd. For I had known it all my life to be a face with a certain limited range of emotional expression. I did not recognize the looks she was beginning to give my inquisitive wife.

I saw my mother begin to awaken, against her will. As if from ancient sleep. To shake herself, as an animal after hibernation might do. I saw her rouse her memory. I saw her look down at herself, as if for the first time since girlhood, over sixty years ago, and see all the black clothing shrouding her, and the kerchief, black, in all this Greek heat, tied under her chin. I saw that she feared what might happen to her, under Susannah's curious questions. And that her solution was to entice Susannah into becoming a tourist.

Go to the church, she croaked, pulling us toward the road. Take Susannah to see our precious sites, she said, grinning grimly so that her worn gold tooth showed.

She had made a pun without realizing it. In America one went to see the sights. In Greece to see the sites. Susannah and I smiled as I explained it to my mother, who looked desperate. A look which actually made us laugh, even as we hoped our chuckles would not be perceived as condescending.

The sun was hot. It seemed hotter even than when I was a boy. The stones so hot a glancing footstep caused them to shed their dust. I took Susannah's hand. She was dressed completely in white, her hair lifted off her neck in one thick, coiled braid that accentuated her height and her elegant, gliding walk. In Greece I did not feel too short for her. Men were often short in Greece, and something in our psyches, Susannah said maybe it was an ancient memory of gods and goddesses, revered the stately woman. I felt instead only pride to be stepping out with her.

—

And so they entered the small white church, the shrine of St. Theodore the Merciful with the tiny brown virgin at his feet, and witnessed a ritual Petros had not seen or even thought about since he was a boy: the local women entering the church, pulling their shawls over their heads, praying silently as they approached the large statue of St. Theodore, but then, prostrating themselves, furtively kissing the small virgin's feet. Look, said my observant daughter, poking her husband in the ribs, as they watched the adoration with which the women did this. Look. Look. There (meaning the women's kissing of the brown virgin's feet) is the reason you fell in love with me!

It was in the church that they encountered the dwarf.

Eyes

At first I honestly did not remember her, though I had seen her every Sunday the entire time I was growing up. She was a fixture of the church. In fact, she lived there.

I felt Susannah poking me as the old women rose from their prostrations, placed their waxy white lilies in the urn left for them, crossed themselves, adjusted their scarves, and backed out the door. I thought she meant to ask about their backing out, a sign of respect to the virgin, as I saw it now, though as a boy I thought it meant deference to St. Theodore. But no, she was nodding toward the edge of the sacristy, where a very short woman, the top of her graying head just visible above what in America is called a pulpit, had already begun to sweep away the dust blown in by the worshippers, tourists, and other aimless travelers.

Her name is Irene, I said to Susannah in a whisper. She lives here. She is the caretaker of the place.

Irene appeared to hear my whisper, if not its content, and sent us a black, blazing look.

Her look appeared to scorch Susannah. It was as if she and the dwarf shared a moment of recognition. What I had interpreted as

a black look was in fact, according to Susannah later, a deep gaz-
ing into each other's eyes. A joining. And why was this? Of course
Susannah, the American, wanted to know. Why should an aging
Greek dwarf look so intensely into her eyes? What about the eyes
of all the other passionate-looking Greek women around? And
come to think of it, in Greece it was easy to see why the word
"passion" also denoted suffering. So many of the women, when
they smiled, seemed to smile through tears. It was in the eyes,
said Susannah, wondering aloud if even the women themselves
were aware of this ancient, indelible grief.

She wanted to be introduced. I explained it was out of the
question. That no one actually talked to Irene. Susannah was
aghast. How is that possible? she asked, staring. And of course
she wouldn't speak English, I added.

Oh, murmured my wife, appearing to sink into herself, to actually become shorter, somehow. Oh, she said, as if to no one in
particular, as if, in fact, to throw the words against the hot dry
wind: Oh, but she has eyes, she finally said. And with these
words, as we walked away, defiantly, she turned and looked back.
But the dwarf was nowhere to be seen.

Paradise

After the experience of meeting Irene's hot gaze in the small, cool church, Petros and I walked outside and began to climb the hill that rose behind it. As a boy he and Anand had played there; as a young man he had walked among the rocks with young girls. For them, at that time, the Fifties, the biggest experience of the week, quite frequently, and if you had a girlfriend, was the sunset.

His mother had sent me to the church, a tourist attraction more than anything else, these days, to get rid of the questions about women that I posed. I had begun to embarrass her. And yet, she was responsible for connecting me with Irene. However, Petros cautioned that I should say nothing about her to his mother. That she had no doubt forgotten Irene would be there, and that I would be curious. His mother, he said, would shrug off my questions; she would have nothing to say.

And you, I said, what do you have to say?

Only what the old stories tell us, he said, holding my hand as we stepped along the narrow path. Irene's mother was raped. Her father and brothers chose not to believe this. She was beaten. No one ever again spoke to her. When Irene was born, her mother died. Irene was a dwarf. God's punishment for her mother's sin. She was given at a very young age, as a servant, to the church.

Petros pointed down to the church, which seemed almost a miniature in the distance. Off to the side, *there*, in a separate square, is where her mother is buried. See the flowers on her grave? They are always the same lilies that the old women bring.

The ones from inside? I asked.

Yes, he said.

No one knows how or when Irene learned that that place was her mother's grave. No one was supposed to tell her, just as no one is supposed to speak to her. But somehow, all these years, she has known.

I will tell her that I also know, I said.

Petros smiled at me. Whoa, he said, imitating an American cowboy, his favorite American hero. She knows. She does not need you to know. Don't be an American busybody.

Was it at that moment that I began to draw away from Petros? Suddenly I felt absent from the Greek landscape through which we walked so admiringly. Even the thought of his parents' oil-cloth, identical to one my grandparents in the South had had—a small square of which I had framed and hung on my college dorm wall—could not restore me. We stood watching Irene stomp out of the church's back door, her arms filled with white lilies, re-minding me of a painting by Diego Rivera; her short, stocky form, all in black, nearly hidden from view. She made her way to the most distant part of the cemetery, and then beyond it, until she arrived at a space that seemed empty—by comparison to the reg-ular burial plots, their white tombstones glittering, all around. There in a large urn were the old flowers, which she plucked out. Then, thoughtfully—critically, it seemed, even from such a distance—she placed the lilies one by one in the receptacle. Finished, she ducked around the side of the church and returned with a bucket of water. After pouring the water through the flowers she stepped back, crossed herself, and backed away.

We watched as she entered her own small room at the back of the church, and I heard Petros sigh, perhaps at the thought of her loneliness, as we watched the shutters come together—but not before we'd caught a glimpse, just before the final banging shut, of something that looked suspiciously like bright red window curtains inside.

What was the life of this woman? This woman dwarf? How could she be so punished for what she was? For being her mother's child? For being? And who had cradled her through babyhood? Comforted her through adolescence? Who had instructed her how to serve both her mother and the church?

It is too much! I said in agitation to Petros as we walked home. Back to his mother's beans, rice, salad, and lamb stew.

I agree, he said sadly. And then, with a sudden violence he added, stomping on the ground: I hate this place.

But it was paradise.

Of Course

Of course I speak English, said Irene, puffing on a harsh-smelling Gauloise cigarette. Cartons of Camels, Kools, Lucky Strikes were stacked against the back wall of her room. I speak German, Italian, Spanish, Japanese, as well. Also Latin, but there's nobody left to speak it to.

Susannah was glad that, on principle, she rarely listened to men. Rarely believed, really, a word they said. No matter how much she might love them.

My husband thought you . . . she began—but how to finish the sentence? It hung there between them. In fact, she realized now, Petros had probably thought Irene couldn't speak at all, since no one was allowed to speak to her.

Husbands, said Irene, with a shrug. I see very little of them. It is usually their wives, women like you, she said, with a slight nod, who are curious.

But why are we curious? thought Susannah, as Irene continued to talk, the Gauloise hanging from full burgundy-colored lips, her brow furrowed as she worked on a piece of embroidery that looked like a tablecloth and covered both her knees.

They used to stone women, here, said Irene into the silence, not so very long ago. Did your husband tell you that? That is what the men tell each other, you know, and whisper into the ears of foreign men, when they get the chance to talk together. Ah, women think they want to know what men talk about! Irene scoffed. You can be sure they stoned a great many, before they got their vaunted "democracy" in these parts. From my window I can see one of the stoning pillars. They say that even a hundred years ago, the base of it was still pink from blood.

Susannah rose from her cushion by the door and looked in the direction Irene pointed. There, way in the distance, toward the sea, and glinting bone white against the royal blue, yes, there was a post of some sort.

It goes on today, more than most Westerners would ever guess, said Susannah, sighing. And in some cultures they have written in their religious books the size and shape of the stones to be used. Some are of a special size and shape to break the woman's nose, others to crack her skull. There had been many recent stonings in Saudi Arabia and Iran; a few brave women and men had risked their lives to tell the world about them.

Irene made a face. She was sitting on a cushion also. Hers was maroon. Susannah's green. It was an amazing room. Every inch of it, walls, ceiling, floor, covered with embroidery or needlepoint. One had the feeling of being small, the size of a fly perhaps, and of lying against the bodice of a very colorful, old-fashioned Greek wedding dress.

I am impressed, said Susannah, that you know so many languages.

I am nearly seventy, said Irene. I never leave this place. What is there to do but to know everything that goes on in the world? To know everything, I had only to learn other people's languages, and, with television, learn to read their weary faces.

Susannah glanced at the large television set in the corner of the room. Is it by satellite? she asked.

Of course, said Irene. From here I can see everything, even into the heart of the modern Diana. She made a face. Princess Di. I can see what a mess she's made of her life, but also how she tries very hard to rise to the meaning of her own name. Her name is a life raft, if she would only grab it. Irene shrugged. What would the goddess for whom she is named think of her? She pulled a thread that stuck up from her embroidery and snapped it between her teeth. She laughed, abruptly. Almost a bark.

To be a princess must have seemed like being a goddess, though, said Susannah, thoughtfully. She had a fondness for Diana, whose stricken or glowing face always confronted one, in North America, from the covers of tabloids, at the checkout counters of supermarkets, anywhere you went.

At the time of the courtship, yes, said Irene. She was so young. And after all, he was, her husband-to-be, a prince.

Hmm, said Susannah. I remember when I got it about saints and goddesses. The difference, I mean. Saints are too good to be true, and goddesses insist on being both magical and real. It is because they're good and bad and because with them, anything can happen, that they're goddesses.

Diana was a huntress, mused Irene. She knew everything about getting what she wanted; but as goddess she maintained the freedom to toss back what didn't please her. A mere princess has trouble doing that. She grunted, and tugged the section of cloth she was working on so that it more snugly fit its frame.

The evening was coming on; the afternoon had been hot and dry. Irene served tea festooned with fresh mint leaves and poured over slivered ice.

Susannah sat limply on her green cushion, which she'd dragged away from the door; her back was now against Irene's small wooden bed.

There are also wonderful tapes, said Irene. But best of all are the soap operas. In every nationality they are the best way to learn a language.

No kidding? said Susannah, sipping her tea.

No kidding, said Irene, mocking Susannah's tone, but with her own amusing, to Susannah, accent.

But why do women come to you? asked Susannah. And, more important, why do you receive them?

Myself, said the dwarf, pointing to her rounded chest, I think they are drawn by my red curtains.

I certainly was, said Susannah, smiling.

Why does it surprise you that I, even I, should have a thirst for life? said Irene. A woman living alone. A small woman. A very small woman. In a room in back of a white church. A very white church, because I whitewash it every year. In a room with red curtains.

The very description is intriguing, you have to admit! said Susannah, laughing.

And yet Petros had not been intrigued. Nor even interested.

She's a dwarf, she lives alone. She's made her peace with it. Leave her alone. He had been saddened by Irene's fate, Susannah thought now, without really knowing it.

Why don't you ever leave? she asked.

In the old days, when I was young, it was forbidden. I was beaten if I left. Dragged back. There was no place to go, either. My mother was dead. Nobody wanted me.

It is difficult to sit across from anyone and to imagine that they were not wanted. The truth of what Irene said, proved by the life she led, pained Susannah, who still could not quite fathom it. She had been born into a family that wanted her, loved her. But she had somehow discovered a rejecting power in herself, even in childhood, and had used it to shut her father out.

As Irene smoked, and worked on her embroidery, which was a tablecloth that would be sold to tourists, Susannah's mind drifted. She saw her father coming toward her, smiling, and holding out a handful of green-apple jellybeans. He'd carefully removed all the other flavors, because he knew green apple was her favorite. There the candy lay, glossy and fresh, in his large tan palm. They had stopped at a country store as they drove across Texas on their way home from Mexico. He must have bought the candy then.

She felt her hand begin reaching for the candy, and felt her eyes responding to his smile. And then, just then, before she actually reached, she heard June, Mad Dog, Magdalena, clear her throat. She heard her say, though their father had not yet asked her: I do not care for any. And Susannah's hand had remained in her lap, and her eyes had lowered themselves. She heard her father's disappointed Okay, then. And heard him turn away, go around the front of the car, and get in. She'd longed for the taste of those jellybeans! Yet June's cough had made it impossible for her to accept them. Once again she was drawn back to the keyhole. Once again she saw her father turn into a man she did not know.

From the backseat, while her mother and June slept, she had studied the back of her father's head. The way his hair waved, just above his neck, even though it was cut very short. The way his ears stuck out. Theirs had always been a relationship that thrived on touching. In the old days, before she saw him punish June, she would have reached up and run her fingers across the wavy ridges of his hair, and played with the comical stuck-out ears. Now she felt unable to lift her hand. Even though he sat just in front of her, it felt as if he were far away. Only now, as a middle-aged woman, sipping tea with an elderly Greek dwarf during a warm evening on a small island in the middle of a maroon sea, did she wonder what her father must have thought.

Relatives

That night, in bed with Petros, Susannah tossed and turned. Petros thought her restlessness could be calmed by lovemaking, but she did not desire him. The next day she asked if he would accompany her on a stroll that would bring them to the cliffs overlooking the beach. Agreeable, as he almost always was, he said yes instantly. They set out as the air was cooling, and soon reached the stoning pillar that Irene could see from her room. It was made of marble, and leaned to one side. A large metal sign advertising Coca-Cola was propped against its base. There was Greek graffiti scrawled the length of one side.

They used to stone women here, she said to Petros.

I'm sure they did not! he said, looking at her with alarm. Whatever makes you say such a thing?

Women are stoned, you know. Even today. She said this calmly, though she felt herself distancing from the reality of what she described.

Her husband's face had darkened. She felt him draw away from her. Why must you always think of things like that? he said to her.

And is this what you brought me all this way to see? He was angry, not because he disbelieved Susannah, but because he knew there would be no sex now for at least a couple of nights, maybe none for the rest of their stay. And he so liked making love to her in his childhood bed. The child that he had been seemed to still be there in the room, somehow. Looking down upon them making love, a fantasy come true.

She did not tell him that Irene had told her about the stoning post. She did not tell him anything that transpired between Irene and herself. Each day she simply walked to the church, went around to the back, and knocked on Irene's black door.

The next day, as she approached the church, she wondered if Irene had missed her. She thought she probably had not: Irene would be used to tourists showing up, perhaps for several days or even a week or more, but then abruptly disappearing as their boat or plane pulled out. The door was slightly ajar to admit a tiny breeze, sucked in by an electric fan that rotated slowly, and as if searching the corners of the room.

Come in, said Irene.

She was sitting on the green cushion, studying the cards she'd laid out on the floor. Susannah stood over her for a moment, looking down at the spread. It was a tarot deck unknown to her. All red and blue and white.

The colors of our flag, she said, as she settled onto the maroon cushion across from Irene.

Yes, said Irene. Odd, isn't it? It was given to me by a woman from Turkey, who picked it up I believe she said in Spain. It's a Gypsy deck. I don't imagine the cards were so plain in the old days. She slapped down a card whose image was a woman frowning and carrying two huge swords. Oops, she said, time to cut the illusions.

Is that what you think it means? asked Susannah, with the eagerness of her childhood. She loved anything mysterious, not figured out, not yet nailed to the wall.

Irene looked across at her and smiled as she fumbled behind her to grab a package of Camels.

That's what it always means, she said flatly. I will do a spread for you, if you like.

Oh, good, said Susannah, drawing her cushion closer as Irene shuffled the cards. This was awkward for her because the cards were large, and her hands quite small. Still, from years of shuffling them she was expert. They were soon spread in a pattern that resembled a cross. The "time to cut the illusions" card was prominently dead center.

You are on a journey to your own body, said Irene. Not so much your own mind, at least not at the moment; or your heart. But to your own skin, the way it shines, the way it glows, smells, absorbs the light. It is now as if you are embracing a vapor, a cloud, a mist. You are actually someone who left her body long ago, when you were quite young; that is why you walk with such grace and stateliness. You are a statue, really.

Oh, God, said Susannah, who'd always been praised for her walk. You don't stoop over like most tall girls, she'd been told. You walk like a queen.

Irene took up a card with a woman and a man entering an ancient carriage. The man's hand under the woman's elbow. She placed the card alongside her nose and closed her eyes, it seemed to Susannah, carefully. She rested a moment, deep in thought.

Do you know why there is this concept of "ladies first"? asked Irene. It is because, in the early days, if we were permitted to walk behind the man, we would run away. If we were kept in front, they could keep an eye on us. Later on, as we became more tame, they hated to think a woman they desired would only think of running away, and so they invented chivalry. Gallantry. The lifting over puddles, the handing into carriages.

Yes, said Susannah, but what does the card mean aside from that?

There is a man inside you, your own inner man, so to speak, and he is dedicated to helping you. He is lifting you into the carriage of your own body, in which you can begin to take charge of your own life.

Who could that be? thought Susannah. Not Petros?

It is not someone of whom you would think, said Irene, as if overhearing her thoughts. Besides, it is an inner man. Part of yourself. But there is an outer man as well, who calls this inner helper forth.

No kidding, said Susannah.

No kidding, said Irene, mocking her.

I see here, said Irene, holding a card of a woman riding the moon, that you have been far away. You have been lost, really. You have enjoyed being lost, in a way. Being lost means no one knows where to find you. If no one knows where to find you, then you are safe from expectations. In a word, free. That is what being lost sometimes means. But now, it is as if you are calling to yourself. Susannah, Susannah, come back; come home. Irene chuckled. And a little child-woman, far away, sitting I think in a large tree, hears the calling and thinks: Maybe it is time to go back.

—

It was at this point that I could have kissed the dwarf! Instead all I could manage was a gust of wind that blew over the fan. Cards scattered every which way. Susannah exclaimed, What was that!

And Irene shrugged, dragged on her cigarette, and said: The wind. Perhaps the wind is related to you.

I watched my daughter trudge home to her husband's family. Eat a quiet dinner with them. Her thoughtful eyes lingering on the faces of the old man and his wife. Her mother-in-law was not happy that she spent so much time with Irene. Knowing she visited the dwarf almost every day, she still asked not a single question about her. The old man was more curious. He'd heard rumors.

Is it true she keeps a black cat? he asked Susannah, as she toyed with a last sliver of tomato on her plate.

I haven't seen one, actually, she said.

And does she make a brew of bitter herbs that she tries to pass off as medicine?

No, said Susannah, laughing. She makes and serves tea.

And can she send her mind out traveling on the currents of the night vibrations?

No, said Susannah, she has television by satellite. She also has a computer.

Wealth

My father was wealthy, said Irene the next time they talked. Not as wealthy as Onassis. But wealthy enough to buy this church for me to serve and to live in.

So you knew him, said Susannah.

An island so small, said Irene, her cigarette dangling as she gutted a fish, of course I would know him, eventually. He was a large, mean, glowering man. I can only imagine what he thought when he saw I was a dwarf. As you can see, dwarves are not common in these parts. Nor are they common any longer anywhere.

Oh, said Susannah, do you think that at one time there were more of you?

We were a tribe, of course, said Irene. Like the Pygmies of Africa. Irene stopped scraping the sides of the fish to look dreamily into the distance. Of all the people on earth, I feel most close to Pygmies, and of course to Gypsies.

Why to Gypsies? asked Susannah, beginning to eat a handful of pistachio nuts Irene had handed her.

Their life is so opposite to mine, said Irene. They go everywhere. Anywhere. They are still a tribe. Every attempt to box them in has failed. I think they must love the earth more than anyone, they are always so willing to see more of it.

Not always willing, said Susannah, chewing. They suffer such terrible persecution for their staunch antibourgeois ways! What they most seem to love is music.

Ah, yes. Music. It is this also that makes me love them. And their worship of the Dark Mother, who is none other than the human symbol for the dark earth.

Or a distant memory of the Pygmy Earth Mother, said Susannah. Do you have Gypsy music, by any chance? she asked.

Irene made a face as if to say: Does a monkey like pistachios?

From underneath the bed Irene dragged an ancient Victrola and a stack of what appeared to be fifty-year-old records. Soon the small room was throbbing with the weeping of Gypsy violins and the deep, soulful laments of Gypsy women and men.

Sighing, Irene said, Why is it that we can love so much that which only makes us cry?

Susannah thought for only a moment, and then, with certainty, she said: Because it is that which calls us home to the heart.

Yes, said Irene, wiping the corner of her eye. I know you must go home very soon now, but I want you to know something.

What is that? asked Susannah.

You are a tourist I like.

Doing Well

When Petros and my daughter left Skidiza, he thought he had loved her back to himself. As they were leaving his parents' house, he gazed upon his childhood bed with fondness. He stood before his parents, his hand tucked underneath Susannah's elbow, and looked them calmly in the eye. He had gone to America with nothing, and had had the good fortune to marry Susannah, a woman of substance, and to find work he enjoyed, and to create a good life. All of the political, cultural, historical forces that had shaped his wife's life remained mysterious to his parents; they simply liked her for her courteous behavior, her deference to their age; they liked her appreciation of their landscape and their food. For her part, Susannah hadn't said anything about the Civil War or civil rights, just as, he realized, his mother had said nothing about the lack of women's rights, historically, in Greece, or about the stoning and stabbing of women she must remember quite vividly from her girlhood. The right of the males in the family to kill the females if they in any way "dishonored" them. They met on the surface of things, but also, in a way, heart to heart. He, Petros, was the place at which they joined.

His parents had been amazed by how well he looked. How handsome and fit. That he spoke English so effortlessly. Susannah was doing something very right, they felt.

And yet, Susannah had stood immobile, as he grasped her elbow. There had been no answering nudge, no shiver from her body to his body suggesting a giggle of solidarity, as his parents praised his good fortune, or even a hint of sadness that they were leaving. He felt that his home, his village, his country, was a sad place for her. That she was profoundly disappointed, and had become estranged from him because of that. He blamed the dwarf. No wonder they made her stay in back of the church, he thought, ungenerously.

Piercings

I am very fat, it's true. And within a year I will be dead because my heart will simply buckle under the strain of pumping blood through so much weight. I teach at a large Eastern university, where I'm sure my students sometimes think of me as Aunt Jemima disguised as Punk Dyke as I come rolling into the lecture hall with my thrice-pierced nose, green hair, and jelly-plump arms filled with their papers, ablaze with my copious multi-colored notes. It is because I teach at this particular university that I am considered a success, no matter what color my hair, how many piercings I have, or how fat I get. I was considered especially successful by my father, who, after my mother's death, used to startle me sometimes when I returned from class, by sitting on my stoop like a stray cat.

What do you want? I bluntly asked him, the first time I found him there.

June, June, he'd replied, with a bit of a twinkle in his sad eyes, have you no pity?

No, I said. And have you come to teach me some?

We did not converse, my father and I, we bantered.

Over time I came to expect his surprise visits. He would take me out to a restaurant, any restaurant I liked, and he would order anything I wanted. Whatever I did want, I wanted lots of it. And I ate and ate and ate, as he watched the plates and platters pile up on the table in front of us in an embarrassing heap. Watching me eat always seemed to take his own appetite away. And I came to believe that each time he visited me, he actually lost weight.

It particularly pained him to see me eat with both hands. And so I would sit before him, a drumstick in one hand, a pinch of roast pork in the other, and I would grunt responses to his inquiries of the day.

—

Am I responsible for this? he asked one day. But I pretended not to know what he meant, and instead asked for the morsel I had my eye on for dessert: a chocolate eclair.

We never talked about his distrust of me. His hawklike spying into my child's personality. We never talked about my fascination with zippers. He had forgotten how it started, if, in fact, he'd ever given it a thought. It was such a small, insignificant thing, and yet how it impacted my life! I said to him once, though: Do you remember that once, the year or so before we went to Mexico, you gave me a little change purse?

Oh, he said, did I? He brightened. Perhaps at my tone of civility.

Yes, I said, you did. It was small and round and black, or maybe dark brown. I don't remember the color, actually, I said, pausing. I was eating a banana split. Some of my students came into the ice cream parlor and I waved to them. My father looked over at them and smiled that courtly smile men of color of a certain age have perfected. It crushed something in me sometimes to ac-knowledge how handsome my father was. To know that straight women adored him and gay men hopelessly drooled. From years of spying I knew he was a great lover; he had that incredibly sexy humbleness that had made my mother delight in turning him on. To change my mother's mind, he was never embarrassed to get down on his knees. To beg. Begging, I'd once overheard him tell another man, actually lit up the attractiveness of a desperate lover's face! For him, it worked. My parents were the kind of lovers who thought of making love in terms not of hours but of days.

My voice became bitter. It was a small round purse, I contin-ued, as my father frowned, trying to recall it. And at first I couldn't figure out what it was. You laughed at the look on my face. And then I caught just a glimpse of something gold, some-thing shiny. And I kept turning the little purse about, trying to get to the thing that glinted in the light. And at last you took it from me and you showed me that the little purse had a golden, hidden zipper!

My father smiled.

And you showed me how to open the little purse, and stayed with me while I introduced the wonder of the little purse to Mother and to Susannah. Who thought it was just as wonderful as I did.

My father smiled still. He did not remember his gift, however.

I sighed, into the last of my dessert.

And then, I said, we were off to Mexico. Everything seemed suddenly mad. There were all those boxes to pack and then the movers came and then we were all crammed into the car, and then there was that interminable drive, with you and Mother talk-ing about being anthropologists but having to pretend to be preacher folk. It was all very confusing. But the point was, for me, not simply that I was losing the only home I'd ever known, but that somehow, in the turmoil of leaving, I had lost the little round purse.

I waited to see if anything sank in. My father asked the waiter for coffee, decaffeinated. Nothing had.

Since that time, I said, I have been fascinated with zippers.

Really? he said, and smiled that charming smile.

———

In one of Susannah's novels, the one called *Going Home*, she tells the story of a blond Scandinavian family who one day get into their Volvo and start driving south. They drive through Europe: Holland, Germany, France, and Spain, into North Africa. And as they drive, they note the darkening of the skins of the people, the changes in the landscape. Eventually they reach central Africa. They drive until they come to the middle of a rain forest, or perhaps the middle of a desert. They get out. There are dark-skinned relatives around a fire who rise to greet them. They inform these relatives that they would like to start over.

Moving to Mexico was, as far as my relationship with my father was concerned, a falling away from the home in myself that my father himself represented. Who was this man, masquerading as a priest? Who was this man, suddenly fixated on the evil in me? I did not know. Not knowing, I was always afraid.

Besides, if my father could not remember the beginning of our peculiar journey, how could I ask him to start over? I dreamed about our years in Mexico all the time.

Green

It was unusual for June to call me when she was happy. The subject that most aroused her to converse was her own misery. Susannah, she would gasp, I have the most horrifying pain in my side, just under my left breast, which itself is feeling excessively heavy and damp. My whole body is pulsating with heat, radiant with pain. I would turn from whatever lover I was engaging, and loosen my grip on the phone. How could she bear the suffering of her body, I wondered, a suffering she so carefully, through compulsive piercing (her nipples had small chains dangling from them, her labia a crucifix) and deliberate overeating, inflicted. I would yawn, my lover nibbling at toes or breasts, and try to imagine a body inured to such pleasures.

I was unprepared to hear my sister's sensual chuckle. Guess what? she said. Her voice hoarse with excitement.

What? I asked, curious.

Guess who I met on the plane coming home from a lecture?

Who? I asked. Sitting up in bed, pulling my toes to myself.

Manuelito.

There was a pause as I tried to remember such a person. Such a name. Manuelito. In general, my sister remembered our years in the mountains of Mexico much more clearly than I did. And when we returned to the United States she'd tried for years to make contact with the people we'd left behind. It wasn't possible, of course, they lived too far away from anything resembling a post.

Manuelito, from the mountains, she said, eagerly. Manuelito. You know, the cute boy with the black horse.

I remembered the horse perfectly. He was a stallion and named Vado, a word which means a shallow place in the river, where one might safely get across. And now I sat upright in bed, a thrill running through me. For instinctively I knew this was a name, a person, who represented the place where my sister had been broken. That her place of brokenness lived next door to mine. And that all these years, she had known it, too.

My God, I said, where did you say you met him?

On the plane, leaving Las Cruces.

I didn't know you were in Las Cruces.

I was, she exclaimed happily. And furthermore, I was in first class, because I have by now outgrown coach seats.

There was not a sign of regret in her voice. How could she say this, I wondered, holding the phone out from my ear, envisioning her incredible girth.

He was in first class!

Manuelito, in first class? I had to laugh. His people had lived in tiny mud houses with dirt floors when they weren't actually living in caves. Perhaps he'd become a gangster, I thought.

But no. He was in the Army, said June. The only one of his platoon who didn't die.

Back up, I said, taking a sip of juice my lover had brought and kissing the air toward the door as it closed.

—

It started in the airport, an airport like any other; the same metal detectors, the same lines of people waiting to have their tickets stamped. The same studied casualness about the notion of foolishly flying so high above the ground. At some point I felt eyes on me. And then I did not feel them. And then, as I was strapping myself into my seat, I felt them again. I looked up, and there was a stocky light-brown-skinned man, something about him vaguely familiar, standing over our seats, looking down at me. He, too, seemed to be snagged by a hint of something familiar. I decided to ignore him, and he sat down, joking with the flight attendant that he hadn't seen her face for at least a month, because he'd been at home with a cold and was too sick to fly. She flashed a complacent grin at him and asked if he'd like his usual. He would. By the time we lifted off he'd consumed several small bottles of gin.

After we were airborne, he unbuckled his seat belt and went into the rest room. When he came back, instead of sitting, he continued past his seat and strolled (I turned to watch) the length of the plane. It was then I noticed that he had a limp.

Where you from? he asked as he dropped back into his seat.

I live on the East Coast, I said, shortly. Burying my head in my book.

Whatcha reading?

A book about physics, I said.

Any good? he asked.

Yes, I said. It's by an Indian mystic who went to school in the West. He says there's nothing solid, not even these leather seats; not even this plane; everything in the Universe is moving; he says his people have known this for thousands of years and didn't need Western science to prove it.

I stopped. I feared I had said too much.

I had.

Oh, he said, if you like to read . . . He reached down into his briefcase and handed me a book. My book, he said.

Sure enough, there he was on the cover, in uniform, just as he sat beside me. I could see the scars better in the photograph than I'd been able to in person. His face must have been blown practically off. I could also see his eyes.

I was in Nam, he said. Everybody else in my platoon was killed. They thought they'd killed me, but I'm one tough Injun.

Injun, I thought. Injun. By now I was feeling dizzy. It was as if something were trying to leave my memory by way of my throat. I undid my belt and heaved myself out of my seat. I tottered to the bathroom and in the tiny, pinched space, threw up in the tiny, teacup-sized washbasin.

When I came back he was sucking on another bottle of gin. After which he got up and lurched once more the length of the plane.

Have to keep moving, he said, sitting down again, almost falling into his seat. If I don't, my joints stiffen and lock up on me.

When did you change your name to Mannie? I asked.

He looked surprised.

Why, he said, how do you know I changed it?

With your Mexican accent, I said, and being Indian, surely you were not named Mannie at birth.

He laughed. After I crossed the border, he said, and went to work in a diner near Los Alamos.

I did not like the name Mannie. I could see where such a name had led him. I picked up his book and began to study the photographs inside. He was staring at my hands. I flexed my fingers and peered at him over my reading glasses.

Oh, he said. I was just looking at your hands. Your little finger has a funny little crook. As fat as it now was, a sausage, it still did have that little crook. I flexed it at him. I once knew a girl with a finger like that, he said.

I was riveted on a picture of him accepting a Purple Heart as well as a Congressional Medal of Honor from Ronald Reagan. Is that your family? I asked, pointing to the somber-faced wife and well-behaved-looking children. They were watching the ceremony with some anxiety.

Yes, he said. They'd wheeled me to the stage, but I wanted to walk up to the president man to man. I only stumbled once. I think I stepped on Kissinger's foot. My wife said I almost knocked the president over, but I don't think that's true. Actually I hardly remember what happened, I was trying so hard to stay on my feet. It was like a blur, like climbing a hill and getting to the top and being blinded by the enemy's fire. But somehow climbing down again and realizing you made it but without a clue about what happened or what you were able to do. Did I pull it off with dignity? I asked my family. 'Cause I wanted Mexican people, Indian people, to be proud of me.

How many times were you shot? I asked, as I looked carefully at the photograph that showed him swathed in bandages, lying in a hospital bed.

There was no counting the shots, because I was blown up so bad. I was lifted out of Nam in pieces. I was in the hospital so long that by the time I came out, Nixon was out of office and Reagan was in. I'm put together with wire. That's why I have to keep moving. If I sit down too long, I can't get up again.

Ha, I said. Just like me.

He laughed, and the swoozy smell of gin hit the side of my face. A diet would cure you, he said; it wouldn't be quite that easy in my case.

Curiously, I've never cared that other people see me as obese. But hearing him refer to it, I felt as if I'd been pricked in the side. As if all my air might be let out. Deflated, somehow.

I came across the border looking for a girl, he said. I came to this country when I was real young. I worked for a while driving cattle. I worked in diners washing dishes. Cooking. I kept thinking I would find her. Just by accident one day I thought I might bump into her again. He laughed. I was really a boy. And I knew nothing about the world. For sure, I didn't know this country was so damn big.

It is big, I said.

It was a relief after a while to join the Army. I'd never heard of Vietnam, and I didn't read the papers that much. But then they trained us and before you know it, there we were.

What was it like? I asked.

Hell, he said.

And you left your family behind?

My wife. She was pregnant. This way I could send money home. I could take care of her.

There was Reagan, grinning, clapping the "hero" on the back. Caspar Weinberger looking like a ghost. Kissinger pretending to be moved. "Mannie," crippled, shuffled forward for his medal, hoping not to disgrace his family and his race.

I had begun to cry.

Whatsa matter? he asked drunkenly.

And before I could reply, he started to snore.

—

Dear Mannie, Manolo, Manuelito,

[I wrote, a week after returning home:] This is Magdalena writing from the past to you. Although I have recently seen you, so this is not the past. I was the woman seated next to you on the plane from Las Cruces. The very fat woman with the nose rings and a green streak in her hair who was weeping as she read your book. I know I do not look like your Magdalena. I am three times her size. My green, buzz-cut, sculpted hair is pressed flatter—the bit that remains—than you would ever have been able to imagine it. Even my nose is twice as large as hers was. Since I have been home I have been contemplating dieting, because you suggested it. Will I make progress? Probably not. But you are not my Manuelito, either. You are a tin man busy drowning your human heart. How many people did you kill, Manuelito? Who were they, and did they have faces like your own? Did you kill women who reminded you of me, Manuelito? It is of this that I dream, night after night. Because you and I have both come back to me, the way we used to be, the moment I lie down to sleep.

Dear Magdalena,

This is Manuelito writing to you. Do not think I did not recognize you. I would recognize the smallest part of you, your little finger, no matter how magnified in size. Or how many nose rings or streaks of green hair you have. But I was drunk, even before I got on the plane, and by the time I thought it might truly be you I was in no condition to know it for sure. So I opted out and went to sleep. And when I woke up, you were gone. How did you do that, by the way? You are a large woman, that's true, but with your magical powers, which I remember from the past, you made yourself completely disappear. You were not in the airport. At least, I did not see or feel you there.

I am hurt that you ask me first of all about the killing. It is why I grew so to hate the hippies. Every time they saw a uniform during the Nam years they disrespected it. Once one of them, a woman with long hair and granny glasses, spat on me. It was kill or be killed, in Nam. I had one thought: to get out of there alive.

That's not entirely true. I wanted to protect and save as many of my buddies as I could. Mr. Nixon understood that. Mr. Kissinger. Mr. Laird. Mr. Weinberger. At least, that's what I thought. It wasn't until after I got my medals that benefits for us disabled veterans started to be cut off, and I had to go to Washington many times to remind everybody that we'd lost our health for them, for the American people. And even though I'm put together with baling wire and can't get a job doing anything that requires staying in one place longer than a few minutes, they wanted to shove me back into a nonexistent workforce.

But that's beside the point. I see on your envelope where you live. I will momentarily be at your door.

—

And did he actually come? I asked my sister.

Yes, she said.

And was it good?

What do you mean?

The reunion, I mean.

Well, she said, he wasn't very drunk, only moderately so. We spent our first afternoon together drinking coffee and walking by the river.

From her description of "Mannie" I could imagine them, rolling and creaking beside the river. I had often shared that walk with her, and with my father, when one of his visits to June coincided with one of mine. The people who saw them together wouldn't know what to make of them; they wouldn't even have a clue.

I asked him if his wife knew he was visiting me, said June.

He said of course. He had been faithful to her, except while he was in Nam. And she to him, except during the same period. It was an agreement they had made.

Even though she was pregnant when he left? I asked.

Yes, said June. They both understood she would not be pregnant forever. And the way he was raised, remember, he would
have been considered pregnant, too.

That's true, I said. I had forgotten this. Although my mother
and father had actually written a small book about this aspect of
Mundo life. How pregnancy was considered thoroughly shared,
so much so that during labor the father-to-be took to his bed with
labor pains and all his buddies gathered around him to offer support. Sometimes the father's cries drowned out the mother's.

It is also characteristic of his upbringing that he would not lie
to her about me, said June. God, Susannah, do you remember
how outsiders would come to the village and talk to Daddy and
Mama and shake their heads and say the Mundo were as unso-
phisticated as children? Just because they didn't lie.

And Daddy seemed to waffle a bit, but Mama was steadfast in
her belief that they were more mature than any of the folks who
came to study them, including her and Daddy.

There was a saying among the Mundo: It takes only one lie to
unravel the world. And when our father, wearing his preacher's
hat, said God had said man had dominion over all the earth, the
Mundo men had declared this could not possibly be true. Perhaps, they had said, stroking their bearded chins, it is the one lie
that has unraveled your world.

While my sister talked, I thought about the Mundo, whom I
had not really thought about in years. They had never understood
how woman could be considered evil, either, since they considered her the mother of corn. When hearing of her original sin of
eating the forbidden fruit, they scratched their chins again and
said, even more gravely, Perhaps this is the one biggest lie that
has unraveled your world. The men had not wanted the women to

even hear what they were accused of; they tried to persuade our father not to divulge this horrible secret, even if he claimed he knew. And when the women found out, they were so hurt.

That they could be considered not good had never entered their minds.

To tell you the truth, June was saying, at first this Mannie/Manuelito disgusted me. I kept seeing in my mind's eye the body of the boy I used to love. I kept looking into his stitched-together face, hoping to have it dissolve into the bright, intelligent face of infinite kindness that I had known. His face had been so destroyed that even his eyelids had been stitched together unevenly. And yet, oddly, passersby would not necessarily have noticed anything wrong. Of course no one really looks at anyone anymore, and of course no one any longer looks like themselves. They all have the same perms, the same bleached sidelocks, the same bland skin. Big noses have mostly been left in the surgeon's rubbish bin.

But pretty soon, something began to happen to me. I did begin to recognize my own pretty Manuelito through the mask of his shattered face; to feel the tenderness in his eyes pouring out through his horrible experience of war, and to stain me, as if he gazed at me through blood.

So much blood, he told me. Rivers of it. Huge patches of earth slick with it. How come you and I are still alive? he would suddenly ask, with the accuracy of the very drunk.

I did not know. At some point I grabbed for his hand, my own feeling like a gigantic, rubbery paw, and his feeling crabbed and shrunken and bent. My thighs rubbed together as we walked, the hissing of spandex a constant strifeful music.

Apology

All your life you have the necessary illusion that you know all there is to know about heartbreak. I hate to be the one to tell you about the heartbreak you experience after you die. There I was, shivering on the bridge over which they passed. Her enormous hand cuddling his. Every wire in his broken body zinging with the cold. I had beaten her for loving his young body! If I were not dead already, I would have killed myself.

That night I could do nothing. I was so ashamed of myself I could not even bring myself to spy on them. I know they came home to her apartment; that she ran a hot bath for him in her gigantic Jacuzzi tub; that he dutifully doffed his uniform and nestled his aching body into the mounds of snowy white foam. I hung my head, or what once would have been a head, outside the front door. What was I to do to make amends? A student came to my daughter's door to bother her with work. I placed myself between her and the door. She knocked and knocked on my chest, the sound killed by the deadness of myself as space. When she left, I sank to my knees and, as wind, began a gentle breathing of apology upward and over the transom of June's locked door.

What Is Left

What is left of it doesn't really work anymore, said Manuelito. Them crazy Cong shot it just about off.

I am sorry, I said.

He laughed, suddenly. Who would have thought we'd end up like this, eh, Magdalena?

Oh, I don't know, I said, raising my leg through the folds of my low-cut silk nightie; I think some parts of us still look pretty good. The moment Manuelito had gotten out of the tub and I had dried him and he had leaned down to kiss the ankle of my left foot—and then had been unable to get up again without help—I had felt my spirits lightening. My legs are still very good, wouldn't you say?

Oh, I agree absolutely, he said, leaning over to kiss my knee.

Your lips are fairly unscathed, I said, leaning back in his arms to study them.

Really, he said, poking them out.

Sure, I said. Kissing them with a big smack.

You're beautiful still, he said, just big. More of you to appreci-ate.

We had been hurrying before; now I knew we would take our time. Remember how I used to brush your hair? he asked.

No, I said.

I used to brush it, he insisted. I used to like the way it curled around my fingers. It is curious about the Mundo: some of us have managed to keep our dark skin, so you can tell we are connected to Africa, but our hair is hopelessly straight. Indians have strong straight-hair genes, he said, chuckling.

It won't snap now, I said, as I watched him search for the brush.

Grinning, he placed himself behind me in the bed. Lean back your head, he said. I did. There was the most delicious feeling of rest, just to have my head on his chest. Slowly he began to brush. I thought he might comment on the green streak, but he did not.

It is much thinner, no? he said. Tugging at the length of hair on the very top of my head.

I did not answer. Billie Holiday was singing very softly. Something merry and hip. I feared the sound of her voice would make Manuelito want a drink. It was that kind of music, that kind of voice. But no, he brushed serenely, shifting his body frequently to keep it loose. He brushed for so long, I began to doze. But the moment I did, he laid the brush aside, and I felt his fingers kneading my shoulders and my neck. I felt them brush the gown covering my breasts.

I love big breasts, he said into my ear.

Well, lover, I grew these melons just for you. I said this as I reached up and guided his hands toward each audacious nipple. Very gently, wincing slightly, he removed the chains. And that is how we began.

Every time a lover leaves you and you are still in love with them, you fantasize about having them once more in your arms.

But it is always a fantasy of how it used to be. Your bodies are the same that you had before. Manuelito and I were the same people, but our bodies seemed to be those of two other people. We kissed. We licked. We rubbed. (He deftly removed the spike from my bellybutton.) But mostly we prayed that our strangers' bodies would come to their senses and find each other again. At first it did not seem possible that this would happen. At one point Manuelito mumbled something about needing a drink. I would have died for a burger and fries. But we persevered. I thought I had to find on his body those few remaining places where he could still be quickened sexually. He thought he had to battle to find my center by pushing aside the fat. But when we became very tired, we abandoned strategy. We napped. And when we awoke it seemed to me the energy of the apartment had changed. When we left my bed hours later, both of us were satisfied.

Magdalena, he said as we ate a magnificent breakfast at Burger King, I want to marry you.

But you are already married, I said.

He looked surprised. This made me laugh.

I am married, you are right. And I love my wife, Maria.

Maria? I said. Her name's Maria? Goddess, I thought, how predictable.

There is not the same magic between us, he said, sadly. There never was. Do you know what I believe? I believe there is one soul in all our time on earth that just matches our own. We are always looking for it, moving in its direction, but so often it is never found. He paused. We found each other not just once, but two times! Not just when we were young and beautiful, but even now, when we are like this.

I stuck a french fry into my mouth. Eating with you feels like eating alone, I said.

That's what I mean, he said.

Even so, Maria is your wife. She's been through too much to let go of you now.

What should we do? he asked.

We should be lovers, of course, I said.

But we must tell Maria everything, he said.

Yes, I said, I remember that is your way.

He nodded.

Will she despise us, or will she have pity on us?

I do not know, he said. I have been a drunk for years; it is hard to have pity for a drunk. We are so disgusting over such long and messy episodes of life.

—

For me, for us, I knew Manuelito would stop drinking. Just as I knew I would immediately begin noticing my weight. But like the Manuelito and Magdalena of old, we did not say anything of the sort to each other, and in fact had stiff drinks and a hearty dinner that very same day.

As we were leaving the restaurant, Manuelito, singing drunkenly, and turning first toward me and then swinging his arms up as though to embrace the rising bright moon, was hit by a bus. The bus dragged him for half a block. By the time I got to him, he was gone.

To Be a Sister

And that is why I am coming down the mountain, the place of refuge where I write left far behind me. The guardian spirit I am gradually beginning to feel, which hovers there, left on the oak tree swing. I am going to be a sister to Magdalena, June, Mad Dog, MacDoc, as she is submerged by another flood of pain.

But I am not sad, Susannah, she said when I arrived on her doorstep. Frazzled from the flight, the midday traffic, and lack of sleep, I gazed at her through bloodshot eyes. Big as I remembered her, she seemed now twice her usual size. Her green hair was lank and her nose rings unpolished. But there was definitely something different about her. What was it?

It was a miracle, our finding each other again, but it was not meant to last, she said. I felt, even as we made love, that Manuelito was on loan to me from someplace else. Not just from Maria, his wife, and their children. There was a pause. Actually, she continued, glancing at the bottom of her teacup, I think he was killed in Nam.

Oh, darling, I said, you make it sound like *The Twilight Zone*.

There *is* a twilight zone, she said softly. Where do you think the one on television comes from?

Come on, I said.

Oh, I understand it isn't rational. She put down her cup. But look at the world, she said. Should any of us give a shit that something's not rational? Nothing out there looks rational to me.

So you met him on a plane from Las Cruces. What was he doing? Where was he going?

Oh, she said. Get this. The "job" the government found for him was to make speeches to high school students. Speeches about the Army. About Nam.

Wow, I said.

Right. She said. So there he traveled, a kind of Indian Flying Dutchman, only alighting at home to get drunk, bully his family, and change into a fresh uniform. A nightmare.

Well, what could he possibly tell the youth? I asked sarcastically.

Magdalena laughed. Exactly. There he was in his neat little Army suit. His body stitched together with metal thread . . . did I tell you the metal detectors in stores always went crazy when he passed by? He had a special travel document that he presented to the guards at airports.

No kidding, I said. Still pondering the change in my sister's character. She had eaten nothing since we came from the airport. She's dieting, I thought; perhaps that explained a certain ethereal radiance that surrounded her.

He wanted desperately to tell the youth the truth, of course. He wanted to tell them to run like hell, from him and from anybody else in uniform. But there he was, stuck to his Purple Heart and Congressional Medal of Horror, I mean Honor, like a fly stuck to a piece of cheese.

So what did he do? I asked.

He tried to tell them how to stay alive. That, he said, was his field of expertise. The only thing he felt he knew how to do. But they weren't Indians. They were soft American farm boys and even softer and sillier urban ghetto youth. Besides, he and they knew the military was the only job they were ever likely to get. The farm youth were bored to death with peace and television; the urban youth risked death several times a day just walking to the corner. He would talk to them all morning, then go back to his hotel room and drink.

He didn't know how to stay alive, I said. Accepting the cup of coffee she handed me.

She shrugged. He died singing, she said.

Oh, I said.

Yes. He died singing his initiation song. When we lived in the mountains he taught it to me, and I used to sing it all the time.

Magdalena began to hum, then to sing softly under her breath:

> *Anyone can see that the sky is naked*
> *and if the sky is naked*
> *then the earth must be naked*
> *also.*

I remember that, I said. I almost do.

I'm telling you, I used to sing it all the time. Or hum it. It drove Daddy crazy, which was part of the reason I did it. At some point, I realized years ago, he really did change himself into a priest; it was as if all his Bible reading and acting to fool the Mundo became part of who he was. I used to think of it as his having been overtaken by his ancient reptilian brain.

It was odd, wasn't it? I said. Both Mama and Daddy were atheists.

They were colossal liars, said June. Always spying on the Mundo and scribbling in their evil gray notebooks.

Their work would have been funded today, I said. Some anthropological society, integrated by now, would certainly spring to the aid of such a fresh, spunky, intelligent-sounding black couple, interested in the doings of a mixed-race tribe like the Mundo.

The church enslaved them, in a way, said June. Forcing them to do its work in order to do their own.

It's hard to imagine that they pulled it off, I said. Daddy preaching about stuff he hardly knew, or cared, a thing about. Mama pretending to be pious.

Fucking kept them going, my sister said bitterly.

Oh yes, I said, laughing. You would never believe how long it took me to understand why it did!

Why the Mad Dog Is Considered Wise

I remember when Magdalena asked me why in my tribe we consider the mad dog wise. It was like her to ask such a question. Her little sister, Susannah, hardly asked anything. She was content to trail sedately behind her parents. In truth, her father spoiled her. It was clear he thought her beautiful only when she was moving very slowly, or when she was still. He would gaze at her as if she were a flower, with no more mobility than a flower possesses. Not so Magdalena. She was all over the place, sticking her nose everywhere. All the elders loved her, because she was still wild. They would tell her stories for as long as she could sit still, and she would run errands for them.

The mad dog is considered wise because it has lost its mind, I said. Which is one of the most difficult things in the world to do. Our people take herbs once a year to lose their minds all together, at once. Instead of thoughts, we have visions, and that is how we guide ourselves.

But why would you want to lose your mind? she asked bluntly, frowning. That sounds stupid to me.

No, no, I said. In the world that you come from, people put too much emphasis on the mind. You could even say they have become mind only.

What do you know about the world I come from? she asked.

I will tell you about that later, I said, but right now I want to tell you about why the mad dog is wise.

Oh, okay, she said, putting her hand on her hip and looking up at me.

She was so pretty! Magdalena. Even when we were still only children I wanted to kiss her. Her lips were full and round; in the summer she became very brown, almost black. Her cheeks were like chocolate. I wanted to lick them. Her spirit was bold; whatever she felt never left her eyes.

Mad dogs bite people, she said now.

That is not the part we like, I said. Nor the drooling or frothing at the mouth, nor the fear of drinking water, either. It is only the losing-of-the-mind part.

Aha, she said.

It is a way of saying you must not live too much in your head. It is a way of reminding you to stay in your emotions, no matter how nutty they are; it is a way of saying, also, that craziness has value.

But wisdom? she said. I don't know if I see that.

The elders say you do not see wisdom to recognize it until you are old.

Well, she said, laughing, nobody could ever get as old as them.

Somehow the elders heard of this retort. They found it amusing. And that is when she began to be called Mad Dog. Which her father insisted must be MacDoc. And then even this nickname embarrassed him. He did not understand that Magdalena was what we called a Changing Woman, a natural one, uninstructed and uninitiated, and therefore very rare.

We saw this immediately. Even on the first day they came to our village. It is easy to recognize a Changing Woman–to–be, even in the person of a small girl. She will be the one who appears to look at everything, deliberately. She will be the one who appears to have no shame. For what good would shame be to someone who might become at any moment that of which she is ashamed?

Luck

Even as the bus dragged me, I sang. Though by then I must have been already dead. Among my people this is considered extremely lucky. It means I will continue to sing, to live, on the other side. At least until my tasks are done. That is what the initiation song promises, even though when you learn it you are so young you cannot possibly understand.

> *Anyone can see that the earth*
> *is grandchild of*
> *the moon*
> *and the moon is mother*
> *of the night sky.*
>
> *When you die*
> *this is the song*
> *that will carry you*
> *beyond the river*
> *it is your small craft*
> *it is your horse.*

And that is why my horse's name was Vado, which means a place in the river where it is easy to cross.

I did not want to leave Magdalena, but now, from where I am, I can see that it was a perfect time to go. That I, in pieces, had been saved for her, returned to her. But I was like a limp rag that was temporarily starched by her love. I stood tall for a moment at her side. Long enough to tell her that I, too, understood that we were meant for each other. That what we'd shared was real. For that was also part of her hunger. To know she was not in a forsaken love alone.

Among the Mundo there is the teaching of nonpossession of others. But I left the tribe so young that it was a lesson only partly learnt. The lesson I did learn was that there is one other soul in each of our lifetimes to which we are primarily drawn. It is a body and a soul attraction. When it is found, what one notices inescapably, is that there is no fear of what anyone thinks. You do not say, Who will like this? What offense will we give? You say only Thank Mama (our conception of God) or Thank Luck. Since to us Mama (everything that is) and Luck are the same.

Meat

My father worked in a meatpacking plant when I was a child, I said to Susannah. Even then, the late Forties, immigrants from Eastern Europe and undocumented workers from Mexico were beginning to be offered the dirtier, lower-paying jobs that men like my father held; he was extremely upset by this. Workers who barely spoke English, whom he'd trained on some noisy, greasy machine, soon rose above him at the plant. All his anger and self-pity was brought home to our door. A scratched and scarred door that was so hideous and forbidding, reeking as it did of the misery on the other side, that as a teenager I saved money from my baby-sitting to buy a small can of yellow paint and painted it "sun."

I have often told Susannah of my childhood because she is endlessly fascinated by stories of survival.

How did your mother feed all of you? she asks, her eyes wide.

In our house, I replied, nothing was ever thrown away. Not even bones.

Not even bones, she echoes, whenever she hears this. What could she possibly do with bones?

Make stock, I reply.

Stock? she says, as if it is a word not found in culinary conversation.

Stock, I reply. There was the stock of the stockyard, I explained, that was not far from the meat-processing and packing plant in which my dad worked. But this stock was a broth that my mother used as a base for making soup.

Oh, she says. She might be brushing her long, sable-colored hair, or painting her nails. I might have just fucked her silly.

We were poor, I'd say.

You were poor, she'd echo, as if the concept of not having plenty was one she could not quite grasp.

—

But my father's stereotypical belligerence, hostility, maudlin and abusive bullying were not all there was to him. There was a whole other side, I said. When he was in his right mind, as my mother called it. After he'd bathed and napped and had a good dinner; after he'd reviewed our report cards and found them satisfactory; after he'd forgone a first drink and lured my mother into their back bedroom, he was a father full of funny stories and play. He was a father who loved to repair things, a father who played the guitar.

At this notion of fatherhood Susannah always perked up. Oh, she might say, he sounds great.

I would ponder this, perhaps while caressing the inside of her thigh.

He was ordinary, I think, I might say.

Tell me again about how you got pregnant, she would ask, just as a child might ask for a fairy tale.

It was in the spring, I would begin.

Wait, wait, she would say. If it was spring, we must open the windows. Or, if it was wintertime where we were, she'd say, Oh, if it was spring, we have to light a candle or make a fire. Ritual mattered to her, more than to anyone I'd ever known. I would wait while she raised the window, lit a candle, laid a fire, or whatever.

It was spring, I would begin again. I was fifteen.

Fifteen, she would echo.

Fifteen, I would say.

Do bad things always happen to young girls of fifteen? she would ask.

Don't interrupt, I'd say.

I believe they do, she'd say, breathlessly.

There was a nice man who was a friend of my family. I did not think he was all that nice. I mean, he was okay but if he'd never come to dinner at all I would have been happy.

You mean you wouldn't have missed him?

Right.

Go on.

I'm trying to.

Sorry.

Aren't you going to ask me again how poor we were? I'd ask.

Oh, she'd say. I'd forgotten that part.

Even before the nice man came to dinner and started to stare at me across the dinner table, we were poor. My father worked all day processing and packing meat. He smelled like meat. He brought meat home for us to eat, hidden in his clothes. Actually, the clothes he worked in he left at the packing plant. I never even saw those. He said that at the end of the day they were so greasy and pukey and bloody they could stand up by themselves. At night all the workingmen's clothes were collected and boiled.

Ew, said Susannah.

In winter he wore a big coat; inside it, my mother had made lots of pockets. We would run to him when we heard his key in the door and pull meat from each of his pockets. If he wasn't too drunk and evil, this made him laugh.

How many were you? she'd ask, her brown eyes darkening in anticipation.

Twelve, I said.

Twelve, she'd reply, as if stunned.

Ten children, I'd say hastily.

She would remain silenced by the thought.

Ten children, all with mouths, my mother used to say.

And were you the eldest? she'd ask.

I was near the middle, I'd say. Number four.

How did you avoid being lost there? she wanted to know.

For some reason, this always made me laugh uneasily. In therapy I discovered I had felt lost, but while I was at home I'd considered myself very important. The older children had my parents for parents, I said. The younger ones had me.

Oh, she'd say, puzzled.

I was a mother from the age of five, I said. It happened gradually. Lily Paul, hand me the diaper; Lily Paul, hand me the baby's bottle. Lily Paul, hold Joey. By the time I was eight I could cook dinner while holding one baby and watching over two more.

No, said Susannah, eyes wide.

Your eyes are wide as saucers, I'd say.

Because she was a writer, this description of herself always made her laugh.

But if you were so important, I don't understand why they wanted to marry you off. You were the perfect hired help, except you weren't even hired.

I only really cared about school, I said. It was a passion with me. I would sneak off to school in the morning after I'd gotten the other children out of the house. I'd leave my mother's babies there for her to tend to. Which she was by then too sick to do.

My God, said Susannah, shivering.

The nice man who smiled at me was penniless. A ne'er-do-well. Charming, though. He loved to sit around and drink and play cards with them. There was no way he could support me. He could only impregnate me, and help them keep me at home.

No, said Susannah.

Oh, yes, I said.

When did you figure all this out?

Years later, I said.

The Grimms have nothing on you, she said.

What do you mean? I asked.

This is worse than Hansel and Gretel, she replied. Worse than being cooked and eaten by the witch. Worse than being Little Red Riding Hood.

Even worse than what happened to Psyche or Persephone, I said, drily.

And Psyche's story ended well, said Susannah, a thoughtful furrow across her brow. Eros came to his senses. Their child was conceived in bliss and they named it Joy.

Right, I said. That didn't exactly happen to me.

You're more like Persephone, my sweet, she said, leaning over to stroke my locks. You were destined to be happy at least half the time.

I loved her sweet breath, as if she'd never devoured anything foul. I kissed her. She was everything I wasn't. Tall, graceful, sleek. Beloved by her parents. Well-traveled. She drove an ancient black Jaguar convertible with the top down even when it drizzled. She waxed her legs.

I did not like him, I said. I did not like boys. I had no boyfriend. I was too matronly, really, by the age of fourteen, for any of the boys at school to be attracted to me.

This man was older?

Much older, I said. Twenty-five if he was a day.

What did he look like? she said.

He was handsome, I said. That much I could agree with my parents about. He had a nice build. His color was nice. Brown, like rich wood. The kind of skin that never had a pimple. He smelled good, too. He tried to talk to me about what I was learning at school. His breath was fresh. I just didn't like him, I said, shrugging. My parents liked him. They enjoyed his company. They saw a use to which he could be put.

But all those children already, said Susannah. You'd think they'd run out of room.

There was no more room, I said. But the older children were leaving, being squeezed out of the apartment, really. But you're missing the point. If I could be forced to stay put, no matter how many children my mother and I had, I would be there to take care of them.

I don't think I can even imagine it, breathed Susannah, as she sipped from her glass of iced Campari.

No, you can't imagine it, I said. That is why I have this hangup with you.

Oh, darling, she said, you're so blunt.

Anyhow. He grinned and grinned at me across the table. Babies dropped out of my mother's body every year, like apples falling to the ground. I was there to pick them up as they fell. She got out of the apartment by going almost daily to watch a movie. She had to wear a tight band around her lower body to hold her uterus in place. It was the most amazing thing, I said, that it was only when

I looked back, after years of therapy, that I recognized how shocking it must have been for me to see this old, graying, bent woman, hobbling about the apartment, pregnant every year.

Was there no word of birth control? breathed Susannah, urgently.

Not one, I said. My parents were devout. They thought birth control meant murder.

And abortion was illegal, she said. Imagine.

More workers for the meat packing plant, I said. They could be paid almost nothing. All my brothers worked there.

And did they steal meat?

Mostly to sell, I said. Or to give to the prostitutes they dated.

What about to the women they married?

They refused to marry. Until they were almost old. They'd much rather pay a women for sex, straight up, as they liked to say, and pretend her children looked like the mailman.

No, said Susannah.

Marriage didn't really appeal to any of us, except for the last three children. By the time they came along there were more jobs. They'd gone to school, become educated. Learned from their classmates and television that not all households had to be like ours.

The nice man kept grinning across the table at you, said Susannah, bringing me back to my tale.

Right, I said. By now I was weary of thinking about my life. I wanted to hurry the story along. A frame of mind that exasperated Susannah, my spellbound audience. I sighed. They kept saying to me: Look at this nice bag of sweet potatoes Winston has brought you. Look at the sheet of cinnamon buns. He's sweet on you. Why don't you treat him a little better? How much better could I treat him? Whatever I cooked, he ate his share. I didn't curse at him or throw rocks when I saw him coming. I was damn polite. Too polite. Some people think politeness is an invitation to invade.

Humm, said Susannah.

He helped me baby-sit the children, so that my mother and father could get out once in a while. They'd go to a movie, to the church basement for bingo, or over to a friend's place. We'd sit on the couch and listen to music while the kids played. Or we'd all sit around watching television. He put his arm along the back of the couch. I admit that sometimes I felt like he was some kind of refuge, some kind of shelter. He'd get up and give a kid a glass of water or a piece of bread and I wouldn't have to do it. I was always anemic, I think from birth, and always tired.

How many little kiddies are we talking about? asked Susannah.

Five, I said, that had to be actively cared for.

However did you do that and keep going to school?

School suffered. I kept going, though. I loved my little brothers and sisters, but somewhere in me I realized they weren't my kids. I wanted to learn about geography, where different places were. I wanted to learn how to draw and use a typewriter.

I didn't even know how you got pregnant. Nobody ever told young girls anything. I just knew I didn't like him closer to me than just to sit beside me and lay his arm along the back of the couch. But one day they got fed up with how uninterested I was. My father, my mother, and one of my brothers, whose best friend Winston was, got me drunk. I'd never even tasted liquor before. And they left me alone with him.

I can't believe it! said Susannah. How could they do that. How did they?

You don't remember? I asked.

Tell me again, she said.

It was really like some kind of bogus initiation ritual, I said. For the first time in my life they remembered my birthday, August twelfth, and they had a birthday party for me. My father brought a cake. Winston brought a present. My brother brought tequila. My mother fried a chicken.

The present he bought me was wonderful. It was a harmonica. I'd always wanted one. I couldn't wait to learn how to play it. I left the table the minute we'd finished eating the cake, and started to practice blowing it. I was already dizzy, and a little sick, from the tequila, but I was really, really happy. They were all looking at me in a funny way, but I paid it no mind.

In short, I said, he took advantage of me while I was passed out.

Ah, Persephone! said Susannah, drawing me closer to her side.

Persephone's mother didn't betray her, I said, burrowing my nose in her neck. Persephone's mother missed her daughter. She turned the earth to winter when Persephone couldn't be found. My mother didn't even ask me what had happened. I didn't really know, anyway. When I turned up pregnant she said how lucky I was Winston was around and that he was someone who wanted me.

She Rode Horses

I could never find my tears, when Pauline told me this story. Partly because she was so unlike the Pauline of her tale. At fifty-five she was a powerful, bold, opinionated woman who wore snug jeans, silk shirts, fringed leather vests, and cowboy boots. She had hair like a wild gray fountain. At the women's club she chewed on a fake cigar and played pool with her butt to the door. She looked women up and down with such a shamelessly speculative glance that white women blushed immediately, black women discreetly touched the back of their necks, and children who'd thought they were grown turned around and went home.

You're always on the make, I said to her, a short while after we met.

She laughed. I enjoy the hell out of it, she said. Why should men have all the fun?

But we're trying to change the way women are viewed, I said. Aren't you a feminist?

I guess, she said. But there's nothing wrong with the way I view women. If they look good I view them a little longer. She shrugged. I could look at you all day.

My girlfriend won't like it, I said. Inventing a girlfriend on the spot and surprising myself.

How cute is your girlfriend? she replied.

This was a woman who'd been raped at fifteen?

You don't have to stay raped, she reminded me. In a way it was a step on the path to liberation for me, she declared, but I didn't know that then.

What did you think? I asked.

That my life was finished, of course. There I was, sick as a dog, big as a house. Having to fuck Winston every night.

The life of the most ordinary woman you see on the street is frightening, I said to her.

Men are trapped, too, she said. I couldn't see it at first, she said. They don't see it. Sometimes it takes a lifetime. But I knew nothing would ever happen for me with Winston. I felt nothing hot, warm, or fuzzy when he touched me. I was repelled. He was addicted to me, though; he'd sit looking across the table at me like a dog eyeing a bone. My parents thought this was wonderful. I told my mother I didn't like it. She said a married woman had to do what her husband wanted. And be thankful he wanted it from you and not from some whore on the street.

I was trapped.

She was not a woman it was easy to think of as trappable. She rode horses, drove fast, spoke her mind. She'd taught herself to make cakes while she still lived at home, and sold them in her apartment building and on the street. After that success, she learned to make pies; these sold just as quickly. By the time her son, Richard, was three, she'd saved enough money to run away. Which she did, leaving him with her family while she went off to night school, finishing which she enrolled in and eventually graduated from college and then enlisted in the Navy. Where she learned aerospace engineering and how to track satellites and the stars. All before buying her first restaurant.

How many lives does a poor woman have? I would ask, laughing, as we sipped margaritas in Cuernavaca or ate ice cream in Rome.

As many as Moll Flanders, she'd say. And a black poor woman has at least three more than she did!

Pauline was well-read—literary, one could almost say. Easily stitching her own story to that of women of earlier times. She cared only for the bold, the brave, the brazen. The women who knew they were trapped and resolved to fly out of one trap after the other, full of anger and heightened libido. She didn't know why she liked me, she said. I was no kind of adequate bitch.

But you don't like me, I said to her. You like to fuck me, but you don't like me.

Of course I like you, Suz, she'd say.

Why does it feel sometimes when you make love to me that you'd like to kick my teeth in?

You've had it all, she said. I try not to be jealous of your life. I try not to envy it. But damn it, I want it. I want trips to Mexico when I was little; discussions about culture and primitive art. I want parents who'd never betray me, she said. When I make love to you I'm trying to take your life. Yes.

That's what it feels like, I said.

And why do I feel like you're sometimes handing it over to charity?

We can't help it that you were raised poor and I was not, I said. Besides, my family wasn't rich, we just had enough, and my parents had only my sister and me. But every parent betrays the child, I said. They can't help it.

Is that why you've opted not to have children?

Frankly, yes.

Pauline laughed. My son is wonderful, she said. He grew up to be the most amazing being who ever lived. How about that!

I'm sure it wasn't anticipated.

Hell no, she said. I thought he'd grow up to run guns and do drugs. Instead, he's this gifted mathematician who was snatched up by M.I.T. He lives in a neat, spacious old house in Cambridge and is a great father to my two wonderful grandsons.

He has a wife, too, I said. You always seem to forget.

She's an uptight little bitch, but I give him that. Whenever I visit them I offer her a joint right away, just to encourage her to mellow out while I'm there. Otherwise every time I look at a woman she gets anxious. She's the kind of woman who worries about being sexually attractive to other women. You know the type. She wears these saggy print dresses decked out with a string of her grandmother's rusty pearls. Every hair clipped neatly to its place. The mystery is that my son is attracted to her. But there you have it. Love is mysterious.

But do you think she'd like you if you were different?

Not gay, you mean.

Yes. And not so goddamn *rough*.

But I *am* gay. I *am* rough, said Pauline. It's what got me out of that bedroom with Winston. Would you ask Tina Turner to tone down her wildness onstage just because she made her daughter-in-law uncomfortable? No, not after she found the tits to kick Ike's bony ass out of her life, you wouldn't. She can be just as wild as she fucking well pleases. And so, goddammit, can I. She paused. What are the motherfuckers going to do about it anyway, the ones who run things so fucking badly in this world—take away your Gold Card? Give you cancer? They're likely to do that anyway, no matter how you act.

When you are being made love to by a woman who expresses such thoughts it is as if you are sitting butt naked on the earth. There is no illusion about anything. You don't fantasize and you don't have time to daydream. It's all right up close and personal. If she even thinks you're trying to evade reality, she fucks you so one-pointedly she brings you right back. Puts her knuckles places you didn't even know you could wash. Kisses you so hard you think about Sunday school. Jesus might love you, this you might know, but being made love to by a woman like Pauline puts the love you fantasized about then in new perspective. Obviously Pauline is doing loving like Jesus couldn't and wouldn't. At least not in the version handed down to the adoring and gullible. After being made love to by Pauline you didn't say, as the hot Christian ladies do, Amen; no, you said what the wild Indians say after a powerful prayer: Ho!

The First Thing
That Happens When
You Die

The first thing that happens when you die, is that you have a burning desire to urinate. You have nothing to pee with, you understand, just the desire to do so. Among my people, we are told this is what happens, and so I was not very surprised. It is understood that spirituality resides in the groin, in the sexual organs. Not in the mind, and not in the heart. It is while fucking that you normally feel closer to God. The other time you feel close to the Creator, of course, is when you create something.

The moment I felt the urge to urinate, I felt at peace. I felt at home. I felt I had successfully transited to the other world. I knew my people had truthfully insructed me, and that I was prepared for any adventure that might be mine to have. Right away I encountered the father of Magdalena, a sobbing vapor beside the bus.

It was strange to feel him there. He was utterly fixated on the mangled body I had left.

Señor Robinson, I said, I am okay. When I spoke to him, he became visible to me. He looked up, tears streaming down his face.

Oh, he said, Manuelito. You poor, poor boy.

Now that he had spoken to me, I also became visible to him.

I am not so poor, I said; I have made it to the other side, singing. Among the Mundo this is the best luck anyone can have.

He reached out his arms to me. For a moment we were one small motion in time. If Magdalena had looked where we were standing she would have seen perhaps a wavy pattern in the air. Then we separated.

Señor Robinson hung his head. I did not come here singing, he said. I knew your people said this was important, but I did not believe them.

How could you know, I said. You were raised among gringos who believe everything that is real is seen.

I could have had faith, he said. Faith in your people. They were so gentle, but they were so poor. When you see that people are so poor it is hard to believe they know what they are doing.

You mean if we had been rich, like the *ladinos*, you would have believed us when we said dying while singing is lucky? But we believe there is something more precious than money; that is why we were always fleeing.

What do you mean, you were always fleeing? he asked. It was as if we had forgotten completely the broken body underneath the wheels of the bus. We had, actually. Now, as we swayed off to the side and out of the way of paramedics and policemen, my body there on the ground was of no more importance than a bag of trash. How it had suffered, though. But this wasn't even a thought, simply something I knew.

Don't you remember why you came to study us? I asked.

Señor Robinson screwed up his face. He had died of a stroke. What he looked like was a very, very old and transparent person, with just enough of his looks left to identify the space he occupied. I don't remember, he said.

It was because we were a mixed-race tribe, I said. And yet we managed to have some coherent social and spiritual beliefs. I chuckled. That's the way you described us when you were trying to get funding for the expedition.

Niggers and Indians, the funders had said, who cares whether what they believe is coherent or not. They're both on their way out. His face averted, Señor Robinson recounted this bitter comment to me.

Most of us are, too, I said, laughing. And boy, when we're gone, are they in for it.

I wanted to learn from your people, Manuelito, said Señor Robinson. I went to the best of my people's schools, but what I most wanted to learn my professors were unable to teach me. How to organize life in a better way than the white man has. How to live in a way that permitted others to live as well.

Well, I said, every Mundo person has one thing in common: exactly like the stars, each of us has a history of flight. And it is the periods of our worst suffering that cause us to fly in the same direction and be brought together. This is what disaster—disconnection from the stars—is for. Apparently. And because disaster is always happening, our tribe is always coming together. That is why the Mundo have not yet been destroyed. We are always being remade. Many of us even live in cities, now.

Is it true? he asked.

Yes, I said. We have studied our killers very hard, since the beginning. We believe we are destined, some remnant of us, to outlive them.

Do you know that the Mundo have always sent spies out to live among the conquerors? That this was always our highest form of sacrifice? The Mundo have always needed someone to sit among the killers and to come back and tell us how little mercy to expect. Your culture is very tricky, though, Señor. Sometimes our people have not come back. Sometimes they have become who they watched. With the widespread use of television, we faced a crisis of major proportion.

How did you deal with it? Señor Robinson asked.

The Mundo way with television, I said, is to put it in a room by itself, preferably a closet, and to choose one person a week or month to go and watch it. Then to report back. We have noticed, I said, that some of these spies, too, never return.

Señor Robinson laughed.

Manuelito chuckled. Anyone with the proper spirit can be a Mundo. Gathering together for a moment before they find and destroy us is the hard part.

But how do you know all this? Señor Robinson asked.

Haven't you noticed? I said. After you die, you know everything.

Ashes

Just like a proper Mundo wife, I found myself humming the initiation song, the same one he had been singing, as Manuelito's
body was placed on a stretcher and carried away. I saw the po-
lice go through his pockets, read his bracelet—which specified
the kind of medical attention he required if found collapsed in
a heap—and knew they would contact Maria. The air seemed to
shimmer before my eyes as I turned toward home. I felt the absence of my parents keenly as I squeezed through my front door.
Sighing, I made myself an eye-watering martini and climbed
into bed.

Looking at Susannah across the room from me, it is easy to see
why she was always everybody's pet. There is a smallness about
her, even though she is tall. She is very neat, and sleek. Even
while sitting alone in a big chair she turns her body this way and
that, as if a giant hand is stroking it.

How is the latest affair? I ask her.

Instructive, she says, and grins.

What is it this time? Man, woman, or succulent plant?

She grins wider.

And Daddy thought I was the tramp, I said.

Are you still angry with me? she bluntly asks, which she's never done before. It stops me in my tracks. The ones I am making toward a bucket of chicken in the kitchen.

Why should I be angry with you? I ask.

Oh, June, she says. Come on.

That you were loved and I was not?

But you were loved. Mama and Daddy loved you.

Mama loved me.

Daddy loved you, too.

He did not trust me. How can love exist without trust?

Do you think God trusts us?

Let's leave that troublemaker out of it.

You just never let Daddy forget what he did to you, said Susannah. I know he apologized.

I wanted reparation, I said, not apology.

Reparation! What are you talking about?

I wanted to be made whole again, goddammit! He'd taken the moment in my life when I was most secure in its meaning. The moment my life opened, not just to my family and friends, but to me myself. The moment when I knew my life was given to me for me to own. He took that moment and he broke it into a million bits. He made it dirty and evil.

Sex scared him, said Susannah.

Right, I said, a man who was fucking all the time, and when he wasn't fucking, thinking about fucking.

He *was* a hypocrite, said Susannah. It troubled him that he was.

Not enough, I said.

He tried to make it up to you. When he and Mama finally got some recognition for their work and some money from their books, they sent both of us to good schools. We never wanted for anything.

I wanted for love, I said. For trust. For a father who wouldn't go ballistic just because I was having orgasms with a cute Mundo boy.

He thought you might get pregnant, said Susannah.

If he'd learned anything important about the Mundo, he'd have known that wasn't going to happen. And even if it had, would that have been the end of the world? He was an anthropologist pretending to be a minister. In neither of those professions is it advised to batter the people you want to engage. It is like the conquistadors who came to the new world and boasted that they introduced the cross with the sword. Well, the cross, Christianity, cannot *be* introduced with the sword. Just as love cannot be encouraged by the fist.

Oh, June, she said. How can you hold on to this stuff?

Do you think I enjoy holding on to it? The man wrecked my life, I said.

Well, you tried to wreck mine, she said, hotly.

What do you mean? I asked.

Don't try to be innocent, said Susannah, looking more flushed than I'd ever seen her. You know what I mean.

I did know what she meant.

I loved Daddy, she said. I always loved Daddy. I also loved you. But suddenly, because of that wretched day in Mexico, I had to choose between you.

Nobody forced you, I said.

You didn't force me, said Susannah, you just never let me forget.

It was something awful that happened to your sister; why should you want to forget?

But he was my father, she said, with vehemence. I loved him. You were the one who'd disobeyed him. Which is what you took pleasure in doing all your life. I never disobeyed him. We got along fine.

And because of my sluttish behavior, you lost him, I sneered. Is that the shit you're trying to tell me?

You never let me forget I was sitting in the lap of a monster, said Susannah.

Somebody had to remind you, I said. Otherwise, I added, you'd have just grinned and Tommed your life away.

She rolled her eyes at this. What business was it of yours? she said. He was never a monster to me! Because of you, I lost my father. One half of the love that was due me in this world. She leaned forward in her chair and wiped her eyes. And he was so pitiful, trying to win me back, trying to rekindle my trust. But you were always there to step between us, to say, at the most tender of moments between us, "No, I do not care for any."

Of his bullshit? No, I *didn't* care for any, I said.

But he wasn't offering it to you, not after a long while, anyway, but to me. You made it impossible for me to accept that my father loved me, that he accepted and trusted me.

If you'd fucked around like I did you would have seen how little he cared about your love and trust, I said.

Well, said Susannah, believe it or not, I did have a love life that he knew about. While we lived in Sag Harbor and I was in high school. He never once scolded me. He never once said I was wrong. He took me aside and talked to me about birth control, just as any caring father would.

I had not known this. It hurt like hell.

But even this didn't ease the tension around sex enough for me to loosen up again with him, the way I'd been before that horrible moment in Mexico.

He was a brute, a hypocrite, a liar. And Mama was his moll, I said.

How can you say that? said Susannah.

She should have left him after what he did to me.

But June, she said, she loved him. We were a family. Where in the world would she have gone with the broken heart leaving him would have given her?

What about my broken heart?

As I said this, I relived the moments of being beaten by my father in the small white room in Mexico. It had been very warm, sultry. A limb of a tree arched across the open window, a bird had flown lazily across the sky. The silver disks on Manuelito's belt made dents in my skin. There was blood. I was thinking only of not crying. And of how much I hated my father for making me forsake, too soon, the recent memory of love.

I began to scream.

June, Magdalena, I heard my sister calling me. I had plunged headlong into the tunnel of my own throat. All that I was, was scream. I screamed and screamed and screamed. There was a hammering at the door. There were sirens. There were strange people in the room. I screamed. I threw my bulk about the living room, breaking everything with which I came in contact. I felt my sister's fluttering throat in my hands, felt her sleek head banging against the wall, breaking the frame of a photograph that hung behind her, a photograph of the two of us, our parents' arms about us, tender and secure. Her pretty face the color of ashes, she raised her arm to defend her face from my teeth and I bit it to the bone. There was a stinging sensation in my upper shoulder. I let go of Susannah's throat and dropped like a stone. Magdalena, June, MacDoc, Mad Dog had come home.

Mad Dog Behavior

When I woke up, groggy, in the hospital, I did not care about anything. I thought about my students. What sense did it make that
I taught them for three or four years of their lives and they still
did not know me? That I did not know them? That I might meet
their parents only once or twice in my life? Perhaps at their
phony-feeling graduation. How stupid this seemed to me. I
helped them on their mad rush into adulthood and into a world
that was steadily turning to shit. Had always been shit. Money
was the god of the culture into which they were born, and would
live to hustle and die; I wanted no part of it.

I thought about my mother. When she was dying I used to visit
and read to her. She would doze, and then I would stop reading
and stare at her face. I was trying to remember how it felt to love
her. For I ceased loving her when she abandoned me. There were
moments of tenderness between us, moments of affection. But I
would not have taken a bullet for her, as I would have done before
she fucked herself back under my daddy's thumb. The cancer rav-
aged her, made her lose the luscious body she'd worn like a flag.

A flag that said: *Nation of Woman Representative. Kneel, Male.* And yet, even as she lay dying, no body at all left to speak of, there sat my father, his hands cupping her flat breasts, his hands cupping her heels, his hands cupping her bony knees. His hands cupping her ass. It infuriated me.

How had I lost out? Was it, as Susannah had once said to me, that I had hardened my heart so successfully it no longer functioned, no matter how I might have wanted it to? And is this what happened when someone broke your heart and you insisted on leaving it that way, just to punish them?

The doctor came into the room while I was thinking of Susannah.

How are you feeling, Ms. Robinson? he asked, glancing at my chart.

He looked like a child playing doctor.

You should at least draw on a mustache, I said.

What? he asked.

You look so young, I said.

I'm thirty, he said. Old enough to know what to do.

Be serious, I said.

He looked at me quizzically.

Nobody's ever old enough to know what to do.

He laughed.

How's my sister? I asked.

Well, you didn't quite bite her arm off, he said. But you reached the bone. I've never seen anything like it, he said.

Mad Dog behavior, I said.

The other Ms. Robinson, your sister, explained that you were under stress, that you'd just lost a loved one.

Manuelito. I had not been thinking of him. Now I thought about the way his back glistened in the water when we played in the water of our mountains' shallow streams. The elegant neatness of his waist. His long, mostly straight, slightly wavy hair. His honest eyes. Sweet nose. White teeth. This fucking country had blown all of that up, I thought. Then stuck it back together with a couple of cheap medals and kicked it out into the street. *Motherfuckers.*

I began to wail.

The nurse will be bringing your medication, said the doctor, heading rapidly for the door. He was obviously one of those Western medical wonders who could only deal with the bit of patient flesh he was poking at and couldn't function if the whole thing started to cry.

Along with the nurse came Susannah, her face horribly bruised, her arm in a sling.

How you doin'? she asked.

Did I give you that black eye? I asked.

Yes, she said. And you bit my arm right through to the bone.

I didn't mean to do it, I said.

I didn't think you did. Well, you didn't strangle me to death. I'm thankful.

Remember how they used to write stories about black people who suddenly went nuts and killed somebody, how they always described it as "going berserk"? Well, we have now witnessed firsthand how that could happen.

I'd never heard anyone scream like you did, said Susannah. It was a scream from hell.

It felt like that, I said. Like it had been building up in me for a thousand years. I couldn't stand it that you had been loved and I had not.

Manuelito loved you, said my sister, sighing.

That is why I was screaming, really, I said. I knew what being loved felt like, and then because of some religious bullshit I didn't even subscribe to, enforced by my own father, who didn't really believe it either, I didn't have it in my life anymore.

We were leaving the mountains, said Susannah; you would have lost Manuelito anyway.

Little sister, I said, don't make me bite your other arm.

Right, she said. That's stupid.

You know what I think? I asked.

What? she said.

I think that some things you don't heal from. Not in this lifetime, anyway.

We could try to help each other heal, said Susannah. We could heal each other.

How would we do that? I asked. I'm set in my ways already. Married to my habits. The biggest habit I have is despising the man who gave me life.

That's easy, said Susannah. Try to imagine the father I love, why I love him. Why Mama loved him. Why you loved him before he humiliated you. Don't pin him to that one moment. He was a human being, like you and me. You just strangled me and took a plug out of my arm, but now you're lying there looking like you're sorry. Are you?

I thought about it.

Come on, said Susannah, don't be such a witch. Aren't you sorry?

Yes, I said.

I rest my case.

It's not the same, I said.

Of course it is, she said.

I was a child.

Maggie, please, just forgive the son of a bitch.

This made me laugh.

Memories Are
So Heavy

Ms. Robinson, said my youthful doctor, the important thing is that you must lose weight.

But my memories are so heavy, Doctor, I said.

It isn't impossible, said my sister, sitting at the foot of my bed. I am coming home with you. We'll start your new life together.

Susannah, I said, it is your goodness that nauseates me.

She smiled.

Too bad, Sis. She turned to the doctor. How much weight should she lose?

A couple of hundred pounds would make her feel a lot better, he said. Her furniture would be a lot happier too.

Very amusing, I said. What neither of you realizes, I continued, is that fatness serves a purpose. When I am fat I feel powerful, as if I could not possibly need anything more.

Yes, said Susannah, and you like to butt people out of your way on the street.

What would I have to eat to lose two hundred pounds? I mused.

Oh, lots of things, said the skinny young doctor. My wife cooks stuff for us that has almost no fat.

What do you cook for her? I asked.

I don't cook, he said.

Why's she stuck with you?

Don't pay her any mind, Doctor, said Susannah, smiling her toothpaste-ad smile, showing her perfect little teeth. She was born to bitch.

And bitch I did, the whole week she stayed with me, talking about carrots and colonics. As soon as she left I threw out the juicer she'd bought and hauled my first big marbled steak out of the freezer, mashed my first mound of buttery potatoes. Had my first alcoholic drink. It was as if my memories were lodged in my cells, and needed to be fed. If I lost weight perhaps my memories of Manuelito and my anger at my father would fade away. I felt so abandoned already, I did not want them to go.

Bad Women Aren't the Only Women

My sister sleeps around, I said to her lover, Pauline.

She looked surprised.

She always has, I said, though when we were growing up I never would have suspected she even liked sex. But she does.

Pauline shrugged. Bad women aren't the only women who enjoy sex. Good women have been known to get down. But your sister is completely loyal to whoever she's in love with. As monogamous as a priest.

Being married to the church would suit her just about as well as it appears to suit those imposters, I said.

I'm telling you, priests play around more than your sister does.

My father considered me a whore, I said. But I have had only one man my whole life. I never cheated on him.

I wouldn't say that, said Pauline.

What do you mean?

I'd say you cheated, with food.

I turned my face away.

Your sister falls in love. Period. I think it is with courage, with guts, which she fears she lacks, that she falls in love. It could be with anyone. She does not appear to look first at the genital area. Loving comes before that, not after. She is faithful to the person she's with. Utterly. If she were not, I would not be with her.

How do you know? That she is faithful? I asked.

Pauline chuckled. I have faith, she said.

Our father loved her, I said; he never loved me.

He must have been very confused, she said.

Her hair was short, spiky, and silver. Her eyes candid and dark. Her slender, curvaceous body, in black jeans and a crimson shirt, ageless and attractive. I could see why my sister was in love with her.

She was a woman who would not let you evade the issue. Nor would she evade it herself.

I felt a familiar flash of envy for Susannah. Such a Goody Two-shoes all her life; to end up with this spunky creature!

My own father was confused, Pauline said with a sigh. Almost with languor. My father was very tired and confused. He had to pretend he wanted all ten of the children who kept him chained to a table in a meatpacking plant.

Why did he and your mother have so many? I asked.

They thought it was the Christian thing to do, she said. They thought if they did anything to stop the births, God would judge them harshly. Though how much more harshly he could judge them than to make them live with ten children in a three-bedroom apartment, I can't imagine.

Is he still alive? Do you see him?

Oh, yes, said Pauline. He is someone now whom I never knew before. Someone who grieves that his children grew up without knowing who he really was. Someone who wants to make amends. Someone who's fun, actually. Old and cute. You know the type.

Too well, I said. Bastards.

You have to open your heart to them, eventually, she said. No matter what they've done.

I'll die first, I said.

You might, she said, looking at me hard.

Sticking Out to Here

My mother died of bearing children, I said to Susannah.

This is the part of my hard-luck story that is hardest for her to hear. It is exactly as it is with fairy tales. The saddest part is always when the mother dies, which she tends to do early in the story. We are always grateful that she goes early, because it is so hard to lose her; it is far better to have her death behind us rather than in front of us, as we trudge off to meet our destiny. But I had already tired of waiting for things to change in our house, and trudged off to meet my destiny before my mother died. I don't know if she ever forgave me; my siblings have sworn she did not. I loved her with all my daughter's heart; hearing that she died blaming me for abandoning her caused me to suffer.

—

She began to hate her body, I said to Susannah. It was too fecund by half. Five children would have left her room to move around. She could eventually have caught her breath. With ten this was impossible.

Hard to imagine, even, said Susannah.

Yes. It was obvious that they still slept together, I said, because there was always a baby on the way. But the first time I had sex with a woman, the first time I enjoyed it or could even fathom what the big deal was about sex, I wondered if my mother had ever truly enjoyed herself. Was ever able to relax into it, so to speak, without the worry about another mouth to feed? It would kill me to know she never actually enjoyed it, I said.

But that's possible, said Susannah. Women all over the world have been brainwashed to think sex is not meant to be pleasurable to them, only to the men fucking them. You're supposed to sort of steal your pleasure from theirs. Fucked, isn't it?

Susannah was so ladylike and proper, so elegantly dressed in just the right matching tones, the right fabrics for the season, the right shoes. She knew how to set a perfect table, knew where each knife and tiny spoon went. It was always a shock to hear her curse. Which she did with the same insouciance with which she asked the florist for a stunning fucking bouquet.

—

That's what Gena said. The woman who tried to help me find an abortionist. And who became my lover after the baby was born. She was disgusted that so many women thought sex was just for the man.

Ah, Gena, said Susannah, pulling her silk scarf across her nose.

She was my teacher. She thought I had potential. She tried to help me by letting me study at her house. Right away we talked a lot about sex, because I was almost completely ignorant, though pregnant as anything. Talking about it, hearing her tell why it mattered to her, why her children reminded her of two very special nights, got me interested.

You really didn't know, she said.

How could I know? I knew the mechanics, sure, but not the wonderful blossoming that good loving means. The way you open, and flow, and feel joined to, and at peace with life. To Winston sex was a game he was playing, on me, and that was just fine with him.

Ugh, said Susannah. Thank goodness I never had a lover like that. Male or female.

You're lucky, I said. It leaves you feeling like shit.

And Gena was not, how shall we say, a Sister of the Yam?

No, I said, laughing. She was white. The daughter of Eastern European immigrants who were as racist as if they were home-grown. But she wasn't like them. She was married and had children of her own; she wanted them to know that Gypsies, who were the niggers of the old country, and colored people were okay. She tried to prepare me for childbirth. It's rough, she said, don't underestimate it. It wasn't that I underestimated it, I knew the damage childbearing had done to my mother's body; I just couldn't bear to think about it happening to me. I liked sports. I liked playing basketball and even football with the boys. I was still doing this in my eighth month. She said: Lily Pauline, you can't keep doing this; your belly's sticking out to here.

I couldn't see it, though. As far as I was concerned, I hadn't put a baby in there, I kind of dared one to be coming out.

Very logical, said Susannah, smiling.

It wasn't really, I know that now. Sometimes I see young pregnant women coming into the restaurant. They carry themselves just the way I did. As if their bodies are still under their control; as if nothing has changed in their world. I don't know what I thought would happen. Gena's husband, Richard, used to ask me questions about the baby: What will you name it? Where will it sleep? Do you have a bassinet? I had nothing, of course, only the bed I shared with two siblings. As for naming, there was no one I cared enough about to name a child after. In the event, I named my son Richard, since he was the only person, other than his wife, who'd inquired about him.

And did Richard ever find out about you and his wife?

I don't know. He didn't learn anything from me; that's for sure. Maybe Gena told him. I can't think why she would. She never left him, and always maintained he was a good man. I agreed. Besides, our affair wasn't like any affair you're likely to read about in *Playboy*. It had this incredible nurturing quality; it was the kind of affectionate sex that seemed designed to reconnect me to myself, to keep me alive. However, it was passionate enough so that I learned about orgasms. And once I learned that I could have them, and have them easily, I realized that in at least that one area I was free.

Susannah was sympathetically stroking my knee. That's a thought not often heard, she said.

I know, I said, because the idea of a personal freedom for slaves (which I considered myself) has always been posited as spiritual. That's the freedom my parents tried to sell me. When I tried to commit suicide by ineffectually slicing my wrists, they hauled me off to church. By then I didn't trust them anymore. Nothing they could have proposed would have interested me. The piety of their religion least of all.

I sat there in the second pew looking up at the minister and wondering what he knew about orgasms, whether he had them regularly. Whether he knew, in the biblical sense, the women who frequently moaned and groaned and fainted in front of him at church. I'm sure now that he did, I said.

Orgasmic freedom has been a male right, said Susannah, with any woman they've wanted to fuck, since the beginning of patriarchy.

It is a very great freedom, I said. Once I experienced it, I felt I had been reborn. Now, when Winston hammered away on top of me I thought of myself as a castle with a thick iron door against which his puny member was useless. And then, with Gena, one kiss, the slightest, most feathery breath, opened me like a rose. It was magic, and I was eager to discover if anyone I knew shared it.

And did they? asked Susannah.

For the most part, no, I said. Which puzzled me. Married women I haltingly queried didn't have it. My older sisters didn't have it. My neighbors' daughters didn't have it. And so on. They had the yearning for it, they ached for it, they pleaded and begged for it, they listened to songs that described and promised it, but generally speaking, orgasmic freedom was not something you could assume was had by every brightly painted, sensuously scented woman walking down the street. This was a revelation. That I, lowly me, somehow had this precious thing. I knew instantly what it meant. It meant I was not forgotten by Creation; it meant that I was passionately, immeasurably loved. I started right away to plan my escape.

What kind of cakes did you first make? asked Susannah.

Lemon, I said. The yellow of the lemon cheered me and made my customers think of sunshine and a better life. My door, you recall, was painted yellow also. After the lemon I made German chocolate and caramel, which is an old traditional favorite among people from the South.

And your pies?

Berries, I said. Yams. I learned everything I needed to know from having watched my mother, but also from Gena, who introduced me to cookbooks. In the beginning, when things were warm and electric between us, she helped me cook. My little brothers were my salesmen and each day fanned out across our neighborhood after school. This was before drugs were imported and sold that way. I paid them a dime for each cake they sold; I paid my mother for the use of her stove. I had to purchase all my ingredients out of baby-sitting money. Even so, my profits slowly mounted.

Susannah laughed. A born capitalist!

No, I said. A born survivalist. Gena found out about a program for college-bound slow learners that she recommended me for; it was in another part of town. I wasn't a slow learner, but so far behind in my studies I might as well have been. The program was the only thing that stood between me and being on the street. I went to class at night. I made it to City College in a couple of years. In college I studied business. Eventually I graduated, joined the Navy, got out, worked in restaurants, bought my first restaurant. The rest, as they say, is herstory.

In the Navy, I tell Susannah, I learned definitively that our country is doomed.

Why is that? she asks, though we have discussed my military career many times.

In the military there is no respect for women. No respect for the feminine, whatsoever. And no respect for anyone who is not white. It is as if the world were made entirely for the pleasure of white males, and that is how they behave. I felt completely unsafe among the men designated to protect our country. Some of their orgies and rapes have since become known, though many of their more despicable acts will never be made public. I was lucky to get out alive.

And how did you? she asks.

By reading novels, going to movies whenever I got the chance, and planning a future for my son. My son, who thought he was my brother, because that is what he was told after I left.

Lily Paul

My husband, Petros, was responsible for my first visit to Lily Paul's, an upscale organic soul food restaurant that he'd discovered through friends.

You're not going to believe what I've found, he said to me.

Is it bigger than a breadbox? I asked, laughing.

Yes, he said. Much.

It was.

Lily Paul's was all ferns and gilded mirrors, chandeliers and parquet floors. However, on each and every table there was the same cabbage-rose oilcloth that was on his parents' table in Greece and framed, one tiny square, neatly on my wall.

I laughed when we sat down.

How's that for a surprise! he said, turning pink with pleasure at my joy.

It's wonderful! I said, laughing into his eyes.

Perhaps tonight would end the way our nights out used to end, I thought. We'd eat a good dinner, drink a bottle or two of wine. Ogle each other across the guttering candle, play footsie under

the table with our stockinged feet. Embrace as we left the estab-
lishment. Make love all night long. We needed this to happen. We
prayed it would. It did not.

What'll you have? asked a sexy woman with spiky silver hair.

My wife, answered Petros.

Not a bad choice, said the woman, grinning.

The smile left Petros's face immediately. But the woman and I
maintained our merry mood.

Halfway through a delicious dinner, I felt it only cultured to
thank her for the food and to formally introduce myself. What is
your name? I asked.

I'm Lily Paul, she said. I own the joint.

Oh, I said, impressed. I'm Susannah Robinson and this is my
husband, Petros.

How do you do, she said.

He was not doing well. A pall seemed to have dropped over his
head.

What's the matter? I asked, as Lily Paul went to tally our check.

Dykes, he said. Their boldness takes my appetite away.

Do you think she's a dyke? I asked. What makes you think so?

He rolled his eyes. Be serious, Susannah, he said. Look at how
she carries herself.

Lily Paul was sauntering back to our table, smiling and chat-
ting with customers who stopped her along the way. Her silver
hair radiant under the lights. She looks like she doesn't give a
damn what anyone thinks, I said, studying her. Is it that that
makes her a dyke?

Oh, be quiet, he said. Then, pleasantly, to Lily Paul, he said: A
nice place you have here. With a big grin.

She slipped me her card, and didn't answer.

Two weeks later, I called her.

How are you? I asked.

I'm suffering like hell from menopause, was her blunt response.

Oh, I said, what are the symptoms? Hoping I was not to hear a sad tale about the demise of sexual desire.

Just the usual, she said: hot flashes, migraines, mood swings, bodily aches and pains. Oh, she said, and my girlfriend doesn't want to have sex as much as I do.

I brightened. Shall I come over, I said, and massage your scalp? I've heard that helps.

My scalp belongs to my girlfriend at the moment, just as I'm sure your fingers are in the keeping of your cute husband. He is cute, you know. Something of a phony, though, I thought.

This was such an accurate reading of Petros it made me laugh.

You've got a nice laugh, she said. And you've damn sure got a pretty throat.

I like your silver hair, I said.

We have two places to start, she said.

What do you mean? I asked.

When we make love, she said, we have two places to start: my hair and your throat.

Two weeks later, that is what we did.

Myrrh

Dear Favorite Tourist, the letter began. It was written on the thinnest tissue paper, blue, with a thin, nearly transparent red line running along one side. It smelled of myrrh.

I am writing to you because you were so kind as to give me your address and also because it is true: of all the tourists who have come to visit the Greek dwarf over the years, slyly poking their noses into a misery they do not comprehend, you are my favorite. Is it because you are so brown and so tall? Because your hair coils on the back of your neck like that of a Greek goddess? Or is it because you were someone from far away who joined herself willingly to the unknown, to my poor country, and to my poor country folk? That you came to see me not once, or even twice, as real tourists do, but every day until you left to go home to America? That we became friends?

America. Is it not where everyone wants to be? And is it not paradise?

—

At this, Susannah sipped her Campari, kicked off her slingback pumps, allowed her silky black dress to slip off one deeply browned shoulder, and said to herself, as she settled on a wicker chair in the sunroom: No. No, America is not paradise. This sunroom is, though.

I am writing to tell you stupendous news, the letter continued.

I have left my home, the church! It happened in a way never imagined. Do you recall how I was daydreaming about Gypsies? Pygmies also, but Gypsies, definitely. Well, as life would have it, all of my brothers, to whom my father left his immense fortune, died. Well, they were old men, and it was time. Nothing was left for me, chained as I was to the church. Only after all of them, seven, had died, would I inherit. I wasn't expected to live so long. But live I did. And so, there I sat one day, lolling on a pile of money, when a Gypsy caravan came by. Caravans of this sort, a long line of small, brightly painted wooden houses on wheels, had of course come by my dwelling before; but that was during the years before the war. During the war it was as if Gypsies simply disappeared. Remembered for their tinkering and music and bright, exotic clothing, or for their thieving, lying, and treachery, depending on whom you were talking to. I had the same fear of Gypsies that everyone else had, because their wandering, disorderly ways were regularly, when I was a girl, denounced in our church. So for years I would duck inside my room, lock my door with a beating heart, and peek at them from behind my red curtains. This time, though, I did nothing of the sort. I am by now so old, I thought, what difference would it make if they stole my dinner, stole my money, or even if they stole me? I listened to the little bells that jingled on the red-tasseled reins of their horses; they seemed to be calling out an invitation. To tell the truth, I was beginning to be bored. Learning languages and reading people's

faces on television can be done in any prison. Placing my tiny
derringer in a holster that fitted my armpit, I leaned out to meet
the most colorfully dressed people I'd ever seen. The men wore
fuzzy black hats and embroidered velvet vests. The women wore
long flowery skirts, and gold coins in their long hair. They did not
seem too surprised to see me, actually. They explained that they
were on a pilgrimage that reenacted their former way of life. That
they had built and painted the wagons of the caravan themselves,
and that they were still practicing the songs and music of their
ancestors that they had but recently learned. The older women,
some of them professionals—schoolteachers, doctors, and so on,
in the city—and I were soon telling each other's fortunes, the
men were whittling wooden spoons and drinking plum wine, a
cup of which was offered to me, and the children were running
wild through the cemetery and drawing cartoons on the white
stones. As my old eyes began to take in all this unexpected experience, new life began to stir in this elderly frame. I found myself
swaying to the most soulful Gypsy music; I began, tottering at
first, then finding my own rhythm, to dance. When you have
never danced before, especially if you have never danced before
with others, it is like beginning to fly. Taking my red curtains,
which the Gypsy women liked, and just a satchel of my small
clothes and a belt of money, I locked the door of the church and
went off with them!

At last I was a tourist myself! And traveling with those who
have been tourists for thousands of years. They explained to me
that they were no longer to be known as Gypsies, but as Roma.
That they, like other Indian tribes across the earth, were beginning life anew, from the ground up, by giving themselves a new
and different name. But I will miss the name "Gypsy," I said: to
me it has always meant romance. Yes, they said, but to most people it means being "gypped."

I understood. Each night we traveled across the land, each day we settled long enough to cook, to wash clothes, and to tell fortunes in the town square. This went on day after day. Until I began to perceive a certain relentless quality to it. Why not settle down somewhere? If only for a season? I asked the men and women leading us. And that is when I learned that settling down, for Gypsies, has almost never been allowed. They move on before they are driven on. This was about the most sobering and disturbing thing I'd ever heard. I became morose, rattling along in my red-curtain-covered bed. Listening to the beautiful songs my new friends sang as they trod along the familiar way. They were not at all like birds, as I had thought, free, and forever flying in a new direction, but more like hamsters, always tramping the same long, well-remembered track.

I watched the faces of the villagers through whose streets we passed. Some, the younger ones, were delighted to see a band of people so fabulously dark, colorful, and strange. But the faces of the older people frightened me. It was as if they were looking at ghosts. Many of them surely remembered they'd sent "their" Gypsies to the concentration camps.

At my age, and with my life, you would think a loss of the romantic vision of life would be welcome. It is not, Favorite Tourist. I think the human spirit needs to believe that someone has escaped the general pressing down of life that passes for the male notion of civilization. I had hoped the Gypsies had escaped. But no. One day I was talking to the Jewess writer who has risked so much to bring their story into the light of day; she had friends among our caravan, and she said to me: Ah, nobody knows this, and those who might have known chose to ignore it, but the Gypsies were slaves in Europe, for four hundred years. Bought and sold, humiliated and beaten, killed even, for sport. Forced to work until they died. And I thought, as she spoke, this wonderful young scholar: Just like the black people of my Favorite Tourist! And that is why, this woman said, they are still so cut off from everyone else in Europe, more cut off than the Jews, even after hundreds of years. So insular and so lacking in trust, where outsiders are concerned, that they think all people other than themselves are horribly unclean. Because the behavior of others toward them has been, in fact, unclean and almost always has meant their ruin. The treatment of the Gypsies and of the black people in America, Favorite Tourist, it has been the same, no?

Susannah laid the letter on her thigh, sighed, and looked out the window. A pink damask rose grew close to the sunroom wall. There was a delicious fragrance from the garden. What made the difference between them? she wondered. Between black Americans and black Gypsies? Or between Gypsies and the Nunga (aboriginals) of Australia? Or between the Gypsies and the completely exterminated indigenous population of Tasmania?

Since I have left them, Susannah continued reading, inhaling the myrrh, which I did after a couple of months, I have lived on a yacht, the very one my father used to pick up women from every continent. I do not pick up anyone, but I myself go ashore. I have pressed my nose into every country that lines the seas. I have lived for six months with the little people of the rain forest of Africa, who are just my size, although, in fact, physically they do not really resemble me. Even so, they choose to see me as a grandmother, or maybe a great-grandmother, returning now to them.

But where have I been? I ask through my translator.

I love to ask them this because they cannot begin to imagine my life. They enjoy the photographs I brought along of my boat, but it is difficult for them to imagine me traveling on it; besides, they have never seen the sea.

They say: You went to dig *tuturi* root, far in the farthermost corner of our forest. There you were spotted by the king of nightbirds who needed a helper for his wife. Perhaps your job was to help her gather leaves with which to make aprons, like the ones we wear. Or to help her build leaf houses.

No, I would say, I don't think so.

Then they would shake their heads and shrug. We would all laugh. I might be holding a tiny baby who smelled sweetly of the aromatic herbs tied around its neck, and all around there would be the rustling of leaves and, far in the forest where the women were digging roots, the sound of singing.

This, I thought, was paradise.

But it won't last. How do I know it won't last? Because when you leave the boat to begin the trek into the interior you are surrounded by soldiers. And these people care about nothing but raping young girls and eating food. You are surrounded by refugees, and these people care about nothing but being able to stop, anywhere, to rest. You must wade, literally, through a sea of trash. All of these unhappy people are being pushed toward the forest, where the small people, who so remind me of myself, live. Then there are the sawmills, some of them hundreds of years old. They have been walking about the forest, these sawmills, going from place to place, cutting down the trees with which the little people have always lived. How do I know the future? The devastation I see before me already, everywhere, is how I know.

But you are not devastated, Favorite Tourist, [the letter continued] even though your people, about whom I read—I study them—always seem to be on the very brink of defeat. You are so soft, one feels, and yet perhaps it is the softness of that which bends to the ground and does not break. I imagine you right this minute stretched out somewhere in the sun, thinking of your troubles, yes, but also perhaps savoring a fig. This is the right attitude, I think, Favorite Tourist. Let nothing stand between you and the dance of life. This is what the Gypsies with their everlasting music have tried to do. In the concentration camps where they were killed by the Nazis in vast and scary numbers of which the world has rarely heard, what did they leave to the Germans, aside from the long black hair shaved from their heads for mattress fillings and suit coat linings? A huge collection of harps and violins!

Perhaps I will come to America! My boat is sturdy. It is big and somewhat grandiose, as my father was. Maybe I will come where you are, dock my house in the local harbor, and sail off with you.

Yours,

Irene (E-reen-e)

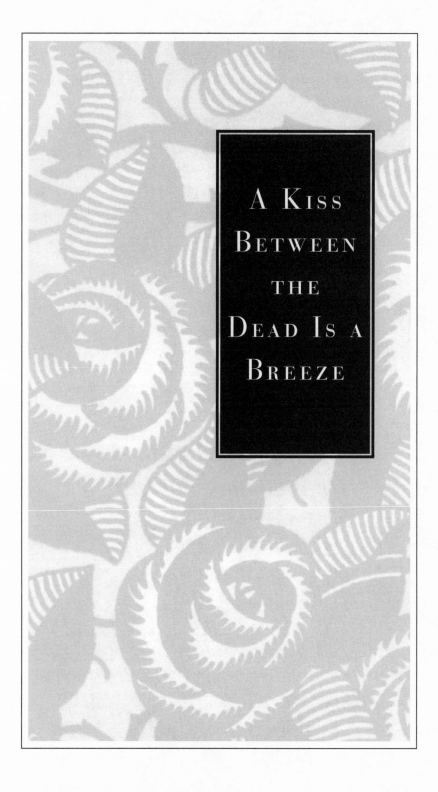

A KISS
BETWEEN
THE
DEAD IS A
BREEZE

The Story You Were Telling Us

The Story you were telling us, Señor Robinson, was strange. Each Sunday you would tell us a little bit more of it, and that very night my father and mother would sit by the fire, pondering. First of all, it was a puzzle why the sun was not worshipped on its nameday, Sunday. Always the Mundo worshipped the sun; it is the god, next to Nature and Earth itself, that is most obvious to everyone. But even though your Story had a day named for it, the sun itself was never mentioned! This was to the Mundo very odd. My parents would repeat what you had said to them, practically word for word, because in our world each speaker is closely listened to. Relatives and neighbors would come to share our fire; the children would use this time to play together, while the grown-ups mumbled and muttered amongst themselves. It seemed too large a story for our parents to handle, is what bothered us. They sat by the fire, poking at it with sticks and regretfully shaking their heads.

While you had run on ahead to introduce them to a hovering god in the sky, which they could only visualize as cloud, they were still worried about retribution from the neglect of any mention of the Sun.

But now, said Manuelito, time is short. I will just talk to you of what to expect from this point on.

He meant, this point of death.

You unfortunately did not make the transition while singing and so a feeling of self-assurance on the path of death is not promised to you. What you are required to do, though, is the same as what I am required to do.

What is that? I asked.

The dead are required to finish two tasks before all is over with them: one is to guide back to the path someone you left behind who is lost, because of your folly; the other is to host a ceremony so that you and others you have hurt may face eternity reconciled and complete.

But Manuelito, I said, I never heard of such a thing!

You never heard because you never listened, Señor, said Manuelito. You have said you came to learn from us, but the sight of us in our poverty sent you straight to your black book. You thought it had all the answers for our situation, when in fact it had none that we could accept without feeling like backward children. Did you really think we did not know we should love one another; that the person across from us is ourself? That stealing is bad; that wanting what other people have is hurtful to us? That we are a part of the Great Spirit and loved as such? What people does not know these things?

We do not believe in heaven or hell, Señor; we do not believe in eternal damnation. We believe only in the unavoidable horror of hurting others and of likewise being hurt. Being sorry and not being sorry. Forgiving or not forgiving. Our Story is one that continues only for as long as it takes us to do these things. We do not know what happens to people after they have forgiven. We do not know what happens after they have proved they are sorry. It is a mystery that we Mundo are happy to leave whole. What we do know is that each of us will have a little bit of time, a window of opportunity, so to speak, in which to make amends, to say good-bye, to bring love back to a love-forsaken heart. And then we are gone, and no one even thinks of us anymore.

As Manuelito spoke, I was thinking of my literal haunting of my younger daughter, Susannah. To her surprise, she was dreaming about me constantly. She was "feeling" a presence lounging and lurking about her house. She was wearing black more and more, as if in imitation of my bogus priestly frock. She was wearing onyx on her finger, jet about her throat. When she slipped into her black car on her way down the mountain, it was as though she were entering me, her dark father, of whom she had once been so proud. So trusting, and so unafraid.

And I, my nose pressed now against the window of her love life, and especially her sex life. Trying to have a place in an area I had nearly destroyed. Was this natural? I asked Manuelito.

It is completely natural, said Manuelito, though perhaps for you it is sometimes very embarrassing. On the other hand, what could possibly embarrass the dead? When you used to tell us in church that God saw everything, we of course thought of him as one of the dead. The recently dead are known among my people as the ones who return to spy on the confusion they have left.

But that would mean that your people believe in ghosts! I said.

Manuelito smiled at me. He was such a handsome boy. Still young; in death, unbroken. Radiant. Not pale and shadowy like me.

To us, Señor, perhaps there is no difference between ghost and angel, angel and spirit, he said. Señor Robinson, he continued gently, do not despair. We understood maybe only one thing about your Jesus Christ: that he was what you call a ghost. That he came back to spy on the confusion he had left. That he stayed only long enough to sort things out. To tell his people not to worry; to absolve them from blame. We were glad to hear he had returned from the dead; this made perfect sense to us. And also we liked him. He resembled a Mundo! Though we never believed he had a physical body that could actually be seen.

The Mundo's Story likewise was created to help us heal the wounds we make while we are alive. Do you know that to us the purpose of Story is to connect the two worlds? We believe your story is what you take with you when you die. And you complete it shortly thereafter. There is a logic in this, I think. We understand that the dead do not vanish at the moment of dying, but continue to talk, so to speak, to weave their story about them, for a while longer. How could this not be so?

You have, though without singing, made it to the other side. I believe I am here to guide you, and I will.

First of all, he said, it is both Magdalena and Susannah who have always needed your love. Of the two of them, however, it is Magdalena who is frail. Her obesity is designed to hide this. Susannah, for all that she seems docile and pliable, an innocent, is a woman determined to have whatever she wants. She is destined to experiment until she finds it. And she is determined most of all to possess her own mind. What this means is that it is in the experiencing of life itself that she finds what she needs. Susannah will survive anything, with the tenacity of a flowering weed. It is my Magdalena, more faithful and more vulnerable, who is dying right this moment of a broken heart.

As he spoke, I could see Magdalena. In fact, I was standing just by her bed, on which she sprawled, mountainous and grotesque. A hunk of chocolate cake in one hand, a can of beer in the other.

What is she watching? asked Manuelito.

But she was not really watching anything. The television was doing a flip-flop and making a droning static-fuzz noise.

I looked closely into her eyes, which were wide open. She seems to be in a coma, I said.

Manuelito sighed. At that moment men in white coats entered the room. They took away her beer and her chocolate cake, drew a sheet over her head, and stood around discussing how to remove her body from the house. They marveled at her weight, and even more at her height. One of the men said something about a horse, and laughed.

I turned to Manuelito. Will she be coming to join us now? I asked.

Not just now, Señor, he said. At least I don't think so. I think she must first pay a visit to her mother, Señora Robinson, your wife.

My wife! I said. Incredibly, I had forgotten about her. Ah, Manuelito, I loved my wife so much, but would you believe, since coming to the other side, I have rarely thought of her!

That is how it is, said Manuelito. That is one way you know that your love was fulfilled. There is no need to think about the loved one anymore. You were with her when she died, no?

Oh yes, I said. I never left her side. She died in my arms. After she died, I said, I kissed her body good-bye. She died of a horrible cancer, I said; her body was in bad shape. It did not matter. It had held her spirit; but I also continued to love it just because it belonged to her. *I* belonged to her. I was a mess myself.

And she loved you?

Yes, I said, I know that she did.

The Mundo have a saying that any real love completes itself. The way that you tell a love is not real is that it is always unfinished. It is just sort of hanging there, maybe throughout your whole life, this ache, this longing.

And why is that? I asked him.

It is because when you truly love someone you wish them no suffering, although they must suffer, just in the course of life. You are always reaching out to them, to heal them. They instinctively do the same for you.

It was like that with us, yes, I said.

Manuelito seemed to smirk. We *know,* he said.

What? I asked.

Did you ever wonder why we bothered with you, Señor? We knew right away that you were a man whose voice was separated from his mind. We needed the protection your presence gave our village, but there had been priests before and we had completely shut them out. You were the only one permitted to stay with us for so long.

I would like to know, I said to Manuelito.

It is because you were always making love to your wife.

If I had had a jaw it would have dropped.

Manuelito chuckled.

You rotten little bastards! I said.

No, no, Señor Robinson, it was not the children who were spying on you! What have I been telling you about the Mundo way of life?

Who, then? I asked.

Naturally, said Manuelito, it was the elders.

The elders? I said. Those old men?

And women. Yes, said Manuelito. You will remember that the elders thought no one was finer than Mad Dog Magdalena. Well, the elder who gave her that name died while you were still in the village. She witnessed your beating of Magdalena. We learned how you had hurt her because our elder told us about it in dreams. But before that, as part of her job as a guardian of the village, she kept watch over you, and told us how it was with you and Señora Robinson. Before her, it was another elder. The Mundo always have elders who keep eyes on the priest. Experience has taught us that these elders should be women, because as women they are less likely to identify with the priests, which we call being sucked into the black cloth.

But this is preposterous! I said.

Manuelito laughed. Some of the people they sent to us would not touch a woman. They did not like a woman's long hair; they did not like her laughter or her breasts; they did not like her smell. We knew those men would lead us straight off the face of the earth.

But you loved woman, he continued. At least, you loved Señora Robinson. You seemed to know that it is when making love that we make life. Alas, you became confused about this when your own daughter followed in your footsteps. Yes, he said, Magdalena knew just what you knew. She discovered this, I am proud to say, with me.

Will you ever forgive me? I asked Manuelito, because I could see it was the only question worthy of our apparently limited amount of time.

There was that slight ripple in the air that meant he took me into his arms. We will have a ceremony, Señor, very soon. Things will turn out well, I am sure.

Sucked into
the Black Cloth

Manuelito did not have to tell me what had happened to me. Why I had gone to study his people and ended up knowing nothing, apparently, about them. I had been sucked into the black cloth.

You know, I said to him, that is such an apt description!

¿Qué? he asked.

Being sucked into the black cloth. I was trained to be an anthropologist. I was an atheist. More accurately, an agnostic. How was I to pretend to know whether God existed, and in what form? And yet, once I took the church's money to come and study you, and once I agreed to "do what I could" toward your salvation in exchange for the church's help, it was as if I had died to myself. I was "sponsored" by something I didn't believe in. I thought I could live that way. What a fool!

If Señora Robinson had left you, you would have died, yes, said Manuelito.

I knew that, I said to Manuelito. You have no idea how I begged her to stay.

We had an idea, he said, smiling.

Sometimes I did not know why she stayed, I said. We both knew there was this growing, gaping hole in me. A void, where there was no belief. As I preached rectitude and chastity to the young women of your village, who never exhibited anything else, at least not in my presence, it became more and more necessary to crack down on Magdalena, who seemed wild by comparison.

You were stuck in your own lie, Señor. That is why your voice, to us, held not one note of conviction. That is why the Story you were telling left us so cold.

But your people seemed to grasp it! I said. The damnedest thing. I never felt I truly had the hang of it, even after all those years. But you all seemed perfectly willing to believe I'd brought the Truth, to kneel and accept the wafer, to go along.

What could we do, Señor? The Mundo everywhere are facing extinction. If there is no one studying us, we are not seen as valuable to the world. The *ladinos* come and capture us, force us to work in the forests and the mines. Rape our daughters and sisters and mothers. Even when we live in caves, high up in the mountains, they have found us.

I think the hollowness, the emptiness in me is what killed my wife, I said.

She was a woman of much life, said Manuelito. Magdalena was like her in that way.

I think she kept looking deep into me, as deep as she could peer, down beyond my "handsomeness," down beyond my sex appeal. Down beyond my begging and clinging. And one day, as she looked, I believe she saw it was as she had feared. That inside I was abyss.

You are weeping, Señor, said Manuelito softly. This is not a necessary activity for the dead.

And then, I said, sniffling, the cancer that swallowed her saw its chance. It pounced. No one could protect her from what she knew. She had spent her life with a man without a center, without belief.

No, no, said Manuelito. A man distracted from his belief. His belief in woman. In the woman he made love to, the woman-to-be who was his own child.

Magdalena was always singing, I said. We were now watching workmen remove the doorframe from her door and wheel in a large cart. Several large men nudged and prodded and pushed her body toward the edge of the bed.

Where do you suppose she'll meet her mother? I asked Manuelito.

By the river, he answered promptly. The Mundo believe that is where all children, when they die, meet their mothers.

The River

She was sitting on a flat stone in the shade of a red boulder. There was a riverbed, but it was dry.

I have been waiting for you, Magdalena, she said quietly. I want to cross this thing, but the song I need is missing from my notes.

Your notebook itself is missing, I said to her.

She laughed. It is quite a surprise to find yourself so completely without the old props, she said. I sit here hour after hour, as I did in the old days, going over my notes, just as I did then. Except they don't exist. Any more than I do.

It dawned on me then what my task was: it was to teach her the song of *vado,* crossing over. That meant my other task would no doubt involve my father, and, I hoped, Manuelito.

I stopped myself in mid-thought. Did the dead have hope?

My life was ruined, I said to my mother, because you did not stand up for me.

Oh, darling, she said, how can you say that?

I can say it because it is true, I said. But don't worry, I will teach you the Mundo initiation song. In spite of everything, I said, looking at the dry riverbed, I want you to cross.

I don't know, she said, frowning, and peering across the river. There doesn't seem to be anything in particular on the other side.

No, I said, there's not.

Then why cross? she asked.

The Mundo would say "because."

Because?

Yes, because you have reached the edge of this side. What else is there to do but to cross?

But one side is like another.

That is true.

It doesn't make a great deal of sense, if you ask me.

Still, you would like to cross, would you not?

Yes, I would.

Why?

My mother thought for a long time. She was a pretty, shadowy woman, her eyebrows very dark in her pale, wasted face. I watched light begin to dawn.

Oh, she said.

Yes? I queried.

Crossing is the point, she said. Crossing is life. Being on one side or the other of the river is *beside* the point.

That is what it means to accept being alive, yes, I said. That is what the Mundo believe.

Your father loved me with all the heart that he had, said my mother.

It was not large, I said.

It was a frightened heart, she said. His people were enslaved people who in fact became slaves. You do not become free again by wishing it.

Why didn't you leave him? I asked. If you had left him there is a chance his heart might have grown.

I was too used to him, she said. It was really very good between us, Maggie, especially before you and your sister were born. We bonded on so many levels! However, taking the church's money under false pretexts, well, it was the one big lie that, as the Mundo would say, definitely unraveled our world!

I laughed. My mother seemed almost merry. A sign of the genuinely loved, no matter how small the heart loving them. I died eating chocolate cake and hating you, I said. I was eager to die. I thought that if I died I could at least have it out with you. Now, I said, none of that seems to matter.

If it doesn't matter, she said pertly, give us a kiss.

A kiss between the dead is a breeze. Umm, my mother said, a gentle dust devil, embracing me.

Anyone Can See That the Sky Is Naked

VADO

Anyone can see that the sky is naked
and if the sky is naked
the earth must be
naked too.

While we were waiting for Magdalena, Manuelito, who never referred to her as June, began to teach me the Mundo initiation song. As I practiced singing, I could see he was sometimes amused by my efforts.

What is wrong? I asked. Am I not doing it right?

There is no right or wrong way to sing, Señor. To be really human is to fully understand this. However, the way that you sneak up on the words and attempt to capture them reminds me of the way *ladinos* sing. They like to perfect things, even singing! Once perfected, of course, singing loses its thrill.

What does it mean to say:

From far across the water your destiny
comes swimming to your soul
and in the branches of the nearest tree
lives the first cousin of your hair.

Ah, said Manuelito, this is a question I also asked the elders. It is a verse that I loved but at the same time it was difficult for me to grasp.

It is about the way you are always moving toward your fate, in life. Like a fish that leaves home a free being and ends up that same day fastened on the end of a line. Someone's tasty dinner in spite of its dreams. As for the rest, the Mundo believe the trees are close relatives, and that the wind itself is a relative and is always caressing its kin, as it were.

Anyone can see that woman is the mother
of the oldest man on earth
is it not then a prayer
to bow before her?

Anyone can see that man is the father
of the oldest woman on earth
is it not then a prayer
to bow before him?

But Manuelito, I said, there are some who believe in parthenogenesis. That woman originally did not need man in order to give birth. That she could create life within herself without his help. And furthermore, there are those who believe that for a million years or so this is what she did.

We did not know her at that time, said Manuelito. If we had, our Story would tell us about her. We know woman and man as equals. Differently beautiful, as the elders would say.

And this stanza, I said:

> *Entering this life one is kissed*
> *in all five of the places*
> *that let in the light.*
> *Leaving one is also*
> *kissed.*

It is simple, Señor, he said. When a child is born it is kissed by both its parents in five places: its ears are kissed, its eyes, its nose, its mouth and the place where life begins. When someone dies, those who intimately love her or him will also kiss these same places.

> *When one prepares to make love*
> *for the first time*
> *mother arrives singing*
> *father is there*
> *sweetgrass and*
> *feathers are brought*
> *eggs are eaten*
> *one is kissed in all five*
> *places*
> *the sweet breasts*
> *are thanked*
> *one is sent to the loved one*
> *blessed.*

I was beginning to get the tune. Slow and dreamy. Tremulous. There seemed to be a vibration in the body this song stirred up. As I sang I felt myself quite moved.

It is this stanza that gave us the most trouble with the priests, said Manuelito.

But it is very beautiful, I said, like all the others.

Yes, he said, but have you really listened to what it is telling you? We explained to them that at the ceremony of joining lovers together we burned sweetgrass to cleanse ourselves and our surroundings. That we used feathers to spread the smoke all around. That eggs were eaten in the hope that the union would be fertile, not just in children, but in ideas, creativity, bountifulness for the tribe. All these things they said they understood. However, they did not appreciate the idea of a mother and father touching the breasts and kissing the vulva and phallus of their grown children, even to bless them. We explained that the kissing was respectful, the lightest touch. But they did not care. Because we practiced this, they raided our villages, hacked off our heads with machetes, enslaved us to work in the gold and silver mines. Burned our children alive.

For some reason this struck me as comically vile.

Why do you smile, Señor? asked Manuelito.

Because it is so stupid. In our culture you can watch men and women sucking on each other all day long on television.

But it was out of this tradition of hypocrisy that you came to us, Señor.

My thoughts turned to my daughter Susannah. When she was little, it was always difficult to know what things frightened her; she was composed, unflappable, even as a child. Stolid in her aura of calm, if thoughtful, repose. However, what frightened her more than anything else that I knew of during her childhood was the discovery one day that the Nuer people, in the unmapped wilds of southwest Ethiopia, forced the women to wear disks the size of dinner plates in their bottom lips. Langley had visited this tribe and brought back photographs.

But, Mommy, Susannah had said, wide-eyed, how can the women talk with those things in their lips? How can they eat?

Langley explained that the women only had to wear them in the presence of the men, and that yes, eating was a problem. From the men's perspective, however, the women's condition assured that the women could barely speak in the men's presence, so heavy was the ceramic disk, and this ensured their silence; also, the women could not eat as fast as the men. Which meant the men ate most of the food.

Susannah had had nightmares for weeks after seeing the photographs. She would stand in front of the mirror stretching her own bottom lip.

What are you doing? I asked her one day.

Pulling on her lip she said: But I can only stretch it this far. If I stretch it further, it hurts.

Lips are like rubber bands, I said. She gave me a look of horror. That is what the dentist once said to me, I added hastily. But actually, the way it is done is simple: first a small disk is put into the hole that has been cut in the lip, then a bit later, a larger one, then a larger and larger one, until you get to the dinner-plate size.

And you call that simple, she had said, with a look of grown-up dismay. She was equally disturbed by the sight of women who were forced to wear heavy iron collars around their necks with what appeared to be an iron penis sticking out in front.

How much does that thing weigh? she asked Langley.

Ten pounds or so, said her mother. About as much as this bag of rice.

Susannah looked stricken.

Why don't the women revolt? asked Magdalena.

By now they are the enforcers, said Langley, sighing. They have no memory or record of a time when they did not wear disks and did not wear iron collars with penises on them.

God, I said, it's pretty damn blatant.

All three of my girls turned to look coolly at me.

Yes, said my wife. While I was there I stayed with missionaries who deplored everything about the tribe. Except these practices. They thought that since the women were the enforcers they had originally dreamed them up and were not oppressed by them. Besides, they said it was these symbols of tribal culture—the disks, the iron collar—that made the tribe unique. I said, But the lips and the necks of the women are raw and infected. And because the collars can never be taken off, their necks are never washed. They shrugged and said they passed out cotton swabs, and gallons of alcohol. The men, as I understood it, frequently attempted to drink the alcohol, with horrific results.

It was wonderful being married to my wife. I had the feeling that nothing of importance ever escaped her interest; that she was as open as a sea anemone to the prickling realities of the world. She was alive in her thoughts and her passions in a way that I had ceased to be.

How do you keep believing in your own thoughts? I asked her. How do you continue to have faith in your own beliefs?

She had been building a fire in the corner fireplace of our dusty adobe dwelling. Shrugging her sexy shoulders, she said: I believe my own senses, she said. I feel others because I feel myself. Nobody would freely choose to slit her own lip. Nobody would freely choose a neck rubbed permanently raw and chewed on by flies. I had to force myself to stay under the same roof with the missionaries, she said. I couldn't join the Nuer because I would have had to classify myself as male to receive any respect, from the men or the women.

Ah, my love, I had said, suggestively, while opening wide my arms, how regally you manage to sit on the horns of any dilemma. I have a small dilemma here that I believe you could help me with. But this was one of the few times my wife absolutely refused to make love. Instead, rising from the hearth, with a weariness in her movements she almost never showed, she gave me what I'd come to classify as simply "the look."

We have heard, said Manuelito, that there are people who, just before the young are to be married, cut them there. In the place where the Mundo kiss.

This is true, I said. Parts of the body are cut off and, with a curse, thrown away.

Manuelito's face was a study in disbelief.

Even our dead do not know this, Señor, he said.

Anthropologists, like the priests and the missionaries, have known about this for a long time. Without protest, I added.

How hard life is to understand! said Manuelito. Death should be much easier, don't you think, Señor?

Crossing

I had never dreamed I would one day have to go to Magdalena's apartment and pack up her things. That she would be dead, and I would be left, the last one of our family, alive. Daunted by the huge pieces of heavy furniture and by the tall piles of gross, unwashed clothes I encountered everywhere, I started by cleaning out the re- frigerator, on the front of which was taped a snapshot of me. Typed above my head were the words "Suffering Makes You Thin."

I stared at the photograph in a trance. The woman in it looked out at me smiling. It was true that she was thin; I noted the bones that showed above the neckline of her black dress. The finger she was pointing at the camera was a bony one. The photo appeared to have been taken at a party; I was clowning. It must have been taken by one of Magdalena's students the week I stayed with her and attempted to help get her deteriorating body in shape. We'd gone to Weight Watchers, to the gym, to a spa. Nothing had made much of an impression on her.

She had simply kept singing. Sometimes audibly, sometimes under her breath. Sometimes humming the melody of the song she had learned in her youth. The song Manuelito taught her.

One day, weighing her, we noticed she had lost two whole pounds. I'd clapped my hands and said merrily, thoughtlessly, stupidly: You see, suffering makes you thin!

She had looked at me as if she didn't care if she ever saw me again.

In the end, I hired movers to clear out Magdalena's stuff. I gave her clothes and furnishings to charities. I gave her papers to the university where she had taught. I kept the copies of our parents' anthropological articles that they'd published in the Fifties.

It saddened me that Magdalena had died alone. Was she singing? I wondered. Which was all she seemed at the end to hope for. I asked this question of the men who were first on the scene; men in white coats, distracted and brusque. They did not want to tell me at first how she was found. A can of beer locked in one hand, a hunk of chocolate cake squashed in the other. The sweet and the sour, commingling forever in her mouth. No, if she was stuffing her face, she couldn't have been singing, they finally said.

Closing the apartment for the last time, removing her galoshes and umbrella from beside the door, tossing them into the trash as I walked down the street, I felt an emptiness, a lightness actually, that was not unpleasant. I could not pretend I would miss a sister I never really had. Ours had been a sistership that was fatally blighted one sultry afternoon in the mountains of Mexico. I would have loved having a sister; but Magdalena wasn't the sister I would have loved having.

A few days after her death I received a package, addressed in Magdalena's loping, rather sloppy hand. Inside there was a photograph of a very cute, young Manuelito riding Vado, and a beautiful if crudely made black leather belt decorated with small, oxidized silver disks. There was a letter that began with the stanza of a song:

At the crossing
it is the right way
to release those who
have taken comfort
from our torment.

It is the right way
to leave this place
with a heart
softer than stone.

At the crossing
it is the right
way
to forgive.

It is the right way to release
all hostility toward those
who wound us
by their hapless presence
alone.

It is in forgetting
the trespass
of others
that the vado
at last
becomes home.

Dear Susannah, she wrote, imagine! If the Mundo are right there will be no reason for us to see each other ever again, even after we are dead. Our relationship, ostensibly as sisters, was in fact a relationship of strangers. I successfully killed all sisterly feeling in myself toward you, in any case. Perhaps if people do reincarnate, as some believe, we will find ourselves once again in each other's lives. I will be your butler or you will be my father-in-law.

I tolerated you, but no, I never loved you. Even before your transformation at the keyhole, I thought you were a wimp. You *bored* me, Susannah. Your "goodness," like your thinness, seemed a cowardly hesitation before the banquet life. Of which you should get one, and stop just writing about it. In fact, the letter continued, you are vain and cowardly; the life you have chosen for yourself, trashy and contemptible. . . .

But this is not true, Susannah said to herself as she read, glancing at the long, rambling pages of vituperation still to come. This person, this "other" that Magdalena has constructed to be her rejected sister, is not me. None of my friends would see me this way. Nor is this the way I see myself.

Closing her eyes, she felt Magdalena watching her as she struggled to suppress the love she had felt for her hapless (yes) father. "I do not care for any," she heard Magdalena's maturing voice, as it had sounded that long-ago day in the car. She saw again the green-apple jellybeans, fresh and bright in her father's outstretched palm. Saw herself refusing to raise her hand or her eyes to return his warm look. Saw and then felt herself betray her own love. Among the Mundo the greatest crime one can commit against oneself.

Without her being aware of it, tears were flowing down Susannah's cheeks, off her chin. A pain of loss so sharp it caused her to cry out sent her to the floor. She lay sobbing, pressing her face into the carpet. Like a fool, she had murdered something that had been strong and beautiful within herself, the unconditional love she felt for her father; Magdalena had wanted it to die, and had coldly helped it along. Never caring about the wounds, on both sides, she had left.

Susannah cried until she could cry no more. Daddy, Daddy, I'm sorry, she whispered tiredly. I didn't know what it meant to give you up. I didn't know what it meant not to forgive. And now it is too late!

And yet, just as she was thinking this, she felt Peace itself enter the room. She envisioned it as a naked dark-skinned man holding a bouquet of peacock feathers. He did not stay but swept through, on his way across the room and right through the opposite wall. Humm, said Susannah to herself, rising, and swabbing at her wet cheeks and runny nose.

Was that Daddy before I knew him? she wondered.

Magdalena's letter was still clutched in her hand. Encouraged by her new feeling of serenity, Susannah began to force herself to continue reading it. In fact, she tried to begin again at the beginning. But she discovered, immediately, that there was no need to. She simply felt no interest any longer in anything her sister had thought.

I will not let her manipulate me into feeling the same way that she does about my life or her death, she whispered to herself, feeling more sane than she'd felt in a long time.

Amazingly, because one never thought this is how growth happened, or at any rate, at long last announced itself, in the hushed moment of thinking these thoughts, while blowing her nose on her skirt and not minding the snot, Susannah felt herself complete the process of becoming an adult. She was grown up. She could handle her own life. Magdalena ceased to be a manipulative and mangled psychic twin, stuck to her by pain. Unfinished, the letter slipped from her hands to the floor.

For Every Little
Sickness . . .

How long it takes to understand something! Colonization, for instance, or war. Pauline was speaking passionately through a haze of sinsemilla smoke. Susannah nodded as Pauline passed the joint to Irene. The three women sprawled on velvet cushions on the floor in Susannah's sunroom and the late afternoon sun of a warm spring day lit up their faces and their hair.

So is it true that the CIA helped to drug the black people in America? Irene asked, suppressing a cough and tapping her rounded chest with a pale and fragile hand.

Everyone thinks so, of course, said Susannah.

There was a silence as a bird, just outside the windows, trilled a sweet note.

Pauline laughed.

Susannah looked at her.

I am just thinking, she said, that all over America black folks are having this same conversation, while they are toking away.

Susannah shrugged. It's a natural conversation that grows out of toking.

Yes, I think so, said Irene. I had to give up cigarettes because they were giving me cancer, but I can still toke. Actually, you know, I learned how to toke from the little people. Everywhere they live, every single camp, has its own ganja garden. It grows wild everywhere in the forest, but because the Forest People make camp in clearings where there is sun, that is where you always find the healthiest marijuana.

No shit! said Pauline. And are they always stoned out of their minds?

Irene took another puff. Of course not, she said, exhaling. As with everything else, they use just enough. To them it is a sacred plant, perhaps the most sacred.

Why is that? asked Susannah. If all their plants, the trees, the whole forest, are considered sacred.

Pauline had turned on her stomach and was raptly following the struggle of a large beetle that had flown in the window. Hitting the wall, it had fallen to the floor and now lay on its back, waving its half-dozen orange legs.

A creature as handsome as you must have a mate waiting somewhere, she said to the beetle, turning it over with a finger and urging it to fly off.

It is considered the most sacred because it is the plant that permits humans and trees, nature, to talk. It is the translator, so to speak.

Wow, said Susannah. I always felt that, you know.

Here they claim it leads to crack cocaine addiction, mayhem and murder, said Pauline. But that's probably only if it's grown by peasant slaves in Honduras or Colombia, and all their tears and blood get mixed in with the fear and pesticide.

The perfect ganja, in my experience, said Susannah, is always grown by women. It is always grown with love. It is a plant that responds to feelings.

How do you know? asked Pauline.

Susannah winked. Writers experiment.

I see, said Pauline, dropping the butt as it burned to her fingers.

So your government floods your communities with drugs, horrible ones, said Irene, dreamily, like the British did with opium in China, and then it comes in and arrests the young men for having them.

That's about it, said Susannah.

And then the people with money to invest, invest it in the building of prisons. They've been kicked out of South Africa and other places where their profits kept them in power for hundreds of years. And so all your young men are imprisoned.

Do we really want to go there? said Pauline, sourly, thinking of Richard, her son, and of her grandsons, Bratman and Will.

But Susannah and Irene laughed. You know how you can't get off the stream of consciousness you're on when you're stoned! said Susannah, poking at her arm.

All right, then, said Pauline. Let's fucking play it out.

But having said that she seemed to forget what the conversation was about, as did Susannah and Irene.

They shifted their bodies on their cushions, leaned against the wall of the room, closing their eyes against the setting sun, and drifted into separate reveries.

—

Irene had arrived two days before. She'd docked her boat at the city marina and arrived by limousine at Susannah's door.

Susannah was standing in the doorway of a small gray-shingle cottage, overgrown with roses and night-flowering jasmine.

Although she was expecting a visit from Irene, she was still astonished to see the enormous black car pull up to her gate. Two huge men got out and stood at attention as tiny Irene was helped from the backseat by a third.

Are those bodyguards? Susannah whispered, after she and Irene had briefly hugged.

Yes, Irene said. What a drag it is to have them. But I was warned your neighborhood is not safe.

Not as safe as your church, said Susannah, a bit stung.

Don't be upset, said Irene. I go everywhere with them. She shrugged. I inherited them from my father. They come with the boat. Their fathers used to be bodyguards for him. He was such a reprobate he needed to be guarded.

And you are so tiny, Susannah finished the thought in her mind, that you need to be protected.

Irene was indeed small. Smaller than when Susannah had visited her in her church in Greece. She seemed much older, too, though only five years or so had passed. Her hair was white-orchid white. The lines were deep in her face. Such a good face! Inquisitive and open. Susannah felt her heart warm as she ushered her into her house.

Pauline had been dying to meet her.

I've never met a dwarf before, she'd said. What do I do, bow?

This had made Susannah laugh.

You'll have to bow, just to shake her hand, she'd said. But it's not a big deal. Her small size is not the most important thing about Irene.

What is it, then? Pauline had asked.

Susannah pondered the question. After a moment she said: It is her intelligence, her will. It is also her courage. She has managed to live by herself, *with* herself, for two-thirds of a century without losing her mind.

Oh, I could do that! said Pauline, jokingly.

You could not, said Susannah. And neither could I.

—

And now, as the light faded, Pauline stirred.

In the prisons they force them to work for nothing, she said.

What? asked Irene.

In the prisons where the young men are kept—and young women too, lest we forget—they are forced to work; to make clothing, baseballs, batteries, what have you, for peanuts.

They are a huge pool of exploitable labor, said Susannah.

Why, said Irene, it reminds me of something. Something from television, something from American films.

It's a plantation, said Susannah. The prisons are a contemporary plantation, and what is produced is produced by slave labor.

Our children are in there forever, said Pauline.

Not Richard, said Susannah, warmly. And not Bratman and Will.

Maybe I shouldn't offer joints to their mother, said Pauline, suddenly sober, as Susannah smiled. Seriously. I don't want to be a menace to them. Teach them bad habits.

I believe in the essential goodness of marijuana, said Susannah, even if all the world turns against her. The occasional toke is not a bad habit. Except for idiots.

As I was saying, said Pauline, maybe I shouldn't tamper with my grandsons' mother.

Irene, Susannah, and Pauline laughed.

The only bad thing is that it makes you want to eat, said Irene. But, she said, reaching deep into a bulging string bag that rested on the floor beside her, for every little sickness there is a little cure. Saying this, she pulled from the bag an exquisitely wrapped box of Perugina chocolates. Upon which the three women ravenously fell.

Getting the Picture

I like Pauline [Paul-een-nay], said Irene next day. To get over their hangover she and Susannah walked slowly through the community rose garden, stopping frequently to sniff a fragrant rose.

Although, Irene continued thoughtfully, she is unfortunately named for a man who, through the church, caused extensive oppression of women, although most people are taught that he was all about charity and love.

Who is that? asked Susannah, stopping by a trellis on which a white rose draped its profuse flowers in scented drifts.

St. Paul, of course. The one who hated women so much he demanded their silence in the church and obedience to their husbands forever.

Gosh, said Susannah, and I thought she was named for her father. His name's Paul.

Your Indians here are right to let their children's names come to them long after they are born, said Irene. I learned this is what they do from reading. Everyone's name should be special to them. If you're not careful you can be hauling around a name that insults you every time it's used.

Oh, Susannah, oh don't you cry for me! Susannah began to sing.

Yes, said Irene, I know that song. For I come from Alabama with my banjo on my knee!

Hearing the familiar song in Irene's accent made Susannah smile.

My father used to sing that song to me all the time when I was little. He was dark and dark-eyed. He had a beautiful warm smile. He'd sing it with great enthusiasm, and always while down on one knee.

What a sweet image, said Irene. And the Alabama Indians, did they play the banjo?

Were there Alabama Indians? asked Susannah. And if there were Alabama Indians, I don't think so. How do you know so much more about America than I do?

But of course there were Alabama Indians, said Irene. Mississippi Indians. But not Indians named Georgia, I don't think. Florida ones, though, I believe.

All those names of people, tribes, that no longer exist. People using them and never realizing it. It's chilling.

They were seated now in a bower out of the sun. Irene's breath was short and she was beginning to perspire.

Well, said Susannah, at least Pauline's first name is Lily.

Is it? asked Irene, clapping her hands.

Why, is that good? asked Susannah.

It is the best, said Irene. The lily is the flower of Lilith, the first mother. The rough one who was bored by Adam and went off to have adventures elsewhere. The one before Eve.

Really? asked Susannah.

Yes. It is really, the lily, an ancient symbol for the yoni. People used to think that with just a lily and her yoni a woman could impregnate herself.

You can't be serious!

Yes, and when the Goddess Hathor squeezed milk from her breasts to form the Milky Way, the drops that fell to earth became calla lilies.

So Lily is a powerful name. Perhaps it is the Lily that controls Paul.

Susannah laughed.

It has been the most amazing experience, being with her, she said. She is exactly like some kind of ghetto goddess, in the best possible sense. Someone who's created her own life and lives it to the hilt. However, I think now that our time together is running out.

I am sorry to hear that, said Irene.

Lily Paul wants to get married. I do not. I am already married to a life of experimentation, change. I feel I must try all of life— at least, all of life that interests me—before I can truly understand that all of life suits me. If I marry I'm afraid I'll turn to stone.

That would sound fine in a philosophy course, said Irene, but what is, as you say here, the nitty-gritty? (Neaty-greety.)

Although her own life is perfectly amazing, said Susannah, she wants mine.

What do you mean?

She wants the life she thinks I had. The "idyllic" childhood. The educated parents. The rides in the car. The experience of Mexico. Although we travel everywhere, as the grown women we both are now, and have the opportunity to enjoy it. But it isn't enough for her. She keeps trying to give the experiences she dreamed of as a child to the woman she is now. It doesn't work, and when it doesn't she becomes angry with me. She looks at me and I feel her saying: You had everything in childhood, and now you also have this. It isn't fair!

Did you tell her how you also suffered?

Susannah was surprised by Irene's comment. She frowned, slightly. By comparison with Pauline she did not think she had suffered very much. How do you know I suffered? she asked.

Irene shrugged, a gesture that involved her whole small body and that she had perfected.

Everyone has suffered, she said. In childhood, I would say, everyone has suffered. It is self-evident.

How, self-evident? asked Susannah.

Irene sighed. Look at the world, she said.

Oh, said Susannah.

The other thing is, she said, as they slowly continued their walk, which was now downhill and somewhat easier for Irene, I am metamorphosing into something different, I don't know what yet. But it feels strongly solitary.

I noticed your dress, said Irene.

My dress? said Susannah.

You are all in black, every day. The first day I came I thought it a little odd, that every single thing you wore was black. But now that I've been here several days I see that black has become a kind of uniform. What does it mean?

Susannah stood quite still. Stopped in her tracks by Irene's observation.

When I left Greece, said Irene, I threw away everything black that I owned. Now I wear green, I wear red, I wear yellow and blue.

Yes, said Susannah, I love your new look. You look like the magical person you are.

It was very hard to cast off the black clothing, said Irene. It was as hard to do that as it was to leave my mother buried there behind the church.

You can have her body moved, said Susannah, envisioning a new grave overlooking the sea and surrounded by colorful windflowers.

I will do that, someday, said Irene. I will bring all my friends. We will bury her and we will dance around her grave, and we will shout to the wind that she was good.

I honestly don't know why I'm wearing so much black, said Susannah. I hadn't particularly noticed it. It just seems that whenever I'm getting dressed, black garments are suddenly in my hand. I seem to feel most comfortable in them. Do I flatter myself that they flatter me?

Irene's breath was labored as they approached Susannah's car. Black, like everything else, Irene noted.

Oh, they do flatter you, said Irene. And the way you wear your hair, so short, so close to your skull. However, I miss the long coil that so beautifully accented your head.

I cut it off one day without thinking, said Susannah. I'd had it so long. I wanted suddenly to be free of it.

I'm beginning, I think, to get the picture, said Irene, quietly.

Church

The picture that the dwarf was getting was one I had been getting for a while. My hedonistic daughter, Susannah, the woman who sweetly, docilely, patiently, and with good manners always did exactly what she pleased, going everywhere, doing everything, tasting all that there was to life, was about to leave this way of being behind her. She was about to be sucked into the black cloth.

That night I came to her in a dream. We were in Mexico. But not in the Sierras, where we had lived. We were in a long valley that ran along gentle foothills before fanning out into farmland as it approached the sea. We were riding on the back of a flatbed truck. She at one end, me at the other. We were looking at each other with longing, with tenderness. Between us, in a huge pile, rose a glowing pile of striped, deep green watermelons. As she watched, I slowly took off my long black coat and wrapped one of the melons in it. I banged the melon against the floor of the truck. Then I unwrapped it. Beckoning to her, I squatted with the Mexicans who were also riding in the truck, which suddenly became a church, and we began to eat.

I dreamed about my father last night, she said to Irene, next day.

Was it a good dream? Irene asked her.

It was, she said. I don't remember much about it except we were in Mexico, very together in our feelings, and very happy.

Do you often dream about your father?

Yes, said Susannah. All the time, now. I didn't for a long time. I shut him out when I was little. I closed the door between us. Nobody ever warned me it would take so much energy to keep it closed! Or that I would feel so lonely on the other side.

What is that cry that you sometimes hear in fairy tales? asked Irene.

There's not enough father! They both screamed in mock lament.

I didn't know how little there was until I gave mine up, said Susannah. I hadn't realized it was a luxury to have even the tiniest bit.

My father disowned me, said Irene. The littlest bit of such a noxious parent would have been too much.

And yet you inherited all his money.

And his corruption and his enemies, said Irene. The world sees a billion dollars falling into my tiny lap and it thinks I am made whole by it. What nonsense. My father manufactured arms, his company still manufactures arms, which are sold to poor countries so that the people kill each other. He owned brothels in Cambodia and Thailand. He had poor young children bought and then killed for their body parts. Ugh, she said. It is not possible to pass on clean money when the way it is made is so dirty.

Gosh, said Susannah, shocked. I don't envy you at all!

Nor should anyone, said Irene. I use my father's money to see the world, but that is only a fraction of it. The rest I must disburse in a way that does good.

When my parents went to Mexico to study the Mundo, said Susannah, they needed money very badly. No anthropological society would sponsor them. Things were very racist then. Even more than now. What a difference it would have made if someone like you had been around to fund them!

I think it is ridiculous and ultimately insulting to study people, said Irene. I think you would only need to study other human beings if you were worried you were not human yourself.

Susannah laughed. I've often thought what a European trait studying other people is. Other folk who meet strange people want to dance and eat with them, go swimming and talk about what colorful or peculiar wildlife there is about. They prefer to sit around and smoke ganja or the peace pipe, listen to music and just kick back.

That's because they haven't come to steal everything, said Irene.

Do you think Europeans are actually from here? asked Susannah. They don't seem to like the earth very much.

Where else would we be from? asked Irene.

Oh, I don't know. Another planet, said Susannah. A place where the artificial is natural.

We come from here, said Irene. But remember, we suffered the Ice Age. It came on suddenly, as suddenly as the abduction of Persephone. I've often thought the myth of Demeter and Persephone was a metaphor for the abrupt coming of the Ice Age. We were plunged into the most bitter winter, which for countless generations of our ancestors never ended.

Really? said Susannah.

Yes, said Irene. It destroyed something in us. Or deformed it badly. Something human. It destroyed our trust in nature, our belief that the earth loved us, or was even, really, our home. Everything we loved and relied on had turned on us and treated us with contempt.

Irene laughed, suddenly. And when those frozen Europeans finally stumbled into the warmth that Southern people in America and those in India and Africa had been enjoying while they were freezing, were they mad!

It is so wonderful to listen to you, Irene, said Susannah, because, as you know, generally speaking, white people almost never study themselves. As white people. They prefer to study us and write about how we don't quite measure up.

They can't believe how out of synch they are, said Irene. They can't figure it out and they're afraid to find out how different they are from the rest of the world's peoples. Rather than risk humiliation and have to own up to an inferiority complex, they've spent the last several millennia trying to prove there's something inferior and wrong about everybody else.

Irene snorted. They've catalogued their deviant behavior faithfully, however, on television. It is there for the whole universe to see. Every moment they are destroying something, killing women, and you can't look at the set without having a gun pointed back at you.

What would Tibetan television be like, for instance? said Susannah. Remembering how, in Kalimasa, the puppet show that had once amused crowds of villagers as they gathered around the tiny stage in the middle of the market, had, with television, simply been televised, and that was what the people still loved to watch. Except, eventually, Western movies and TV shows had begun to trickle in, and the scantily clad natives sat in horror as giant buildings exploded before their stricken eyes, and men killed each other over piles of money, and women prostituted themselves for fun, and everybody carried a gun.

The other thing that Europe lost, said Irene, was her mother. Her strong mother.

What do you mean? asked Susannah.

I mean that the men who controlled the Christian Church during the Middle Ages burned her at the stake. The witch burnings, remember?

Susannah sighed. Yes, she finally said, battling an unexpected wave of despair. Imagine your strongest, best, most spirited women—

And wisest, Irene interjected.

And best men, too, continued Susannah. Because the best men always love women. Imagine all of them captured, tortured, and systematically put to death, over a period of centuries!

Irene shivered.

And then these Christian sons of the Inquisition "discovered" us heathens, strolling about in a warm climate, our mothers still respected as midwives and healers, our parents still wise in the ways of plants and the earth.

The Envy! sighed Irene. It gives me gooseflesh just to imagine it. Better to chop off heads and cut Indian babies in half, or destroy black families in Africa by brutalizing and enslaving them—all of which they did—than to realize that much of the "uncivilized" world, unlike Europe, had not been forced to kill off its mother and made to shrink its spirit to half its size.

Living
with the Wind

Like my mother, who was always peering into my father's soul through the aching mist of his love for her, I am always peering through the mist of my orgasm itself. I too am seeking what is essentially beyond it.

Lily Paul looked troubled. To her what was beyond the orgasm was, hopefully, only a brief respite from orgasmic bliss.

No, said Susannah, this does not mean you have failed me as a lover. Quite the contrary, girl. You have been wonderful. You have been the lover to take me closest to the door of my own locked closet.

Susannah laughed, saying this, and met a glimmer of ironic humor in Lily Paul's limpid brown eye.

Thank you, said Lily Paul drily.

Yes, said Susannah. Without our relationship I would never have known how far away I was from what could be. What heights of spirit one might reach through such a physical act. No wonder the church has demonized it.

Thanks again, said Lily Paul. I guess.

Oh yes, said Susannah. I am grateful.

But you do not want to marry me?

If we wanted children, said Susannah. And at our age, what would we do with them?

Ugh, said Lily Paul.

Susannah grinned.

It is astonishing to me that women still have them, said Lily Paul.

Not everyone had your childhood, darling. And even you are happy you had a son. By the way, is it my imagination, or is it true that all pregnant lesbians give birth to sons?

They have more than they'd planned on, said Lily Paul. That's for sure. And there we all are, she sighed, praying for girls. It's enough to make you doubt the Goddess. But aren't you at least curious? she asked Susannah.

About having a child? No, said Susannah. I'd like to have given birth, the same way would-be writers would like to have written. For the experience. I wonder, though, how men can stand it, she mused. Knowing the experience of giving birth is permanently beyond them. Must be quite a blow to the ego.

They couldn't stand the pain, scoffed Lily Paul; they'd faint at the sight of blood.

They've walled themselves off from woman's blood, said Susannah. But how they must miss it! It's what they're made of, after all.

That's why they go to war, of course, said Lily Paul. Why they kill each other.

To see blood? asked Susannah.

To see blood. To experience the awe, the terror, the mystery of it.

They should have just let us continue to drip, said Susannah.

No, said Lily Paul. Birth was too powerful a ceremony. It is the mother of ceremonies for good reason. A trail of blood leads you directly to it. If you erase the trail you can keep people from discovering the ceremony. You can pretend it isn't even happening; or, if it *is* happening, that it isn't really important. You can pretend your ceremonies were not copied from it.

I would be open to a ceremony honoring our true relationship, said Susannah.

And what is that? In your estimation.

You have been my teacher, said Susannah. You have taught me a freer and much deeper expression of sex. I am your student, she said, reaching over to kiss Pauline's hand.

Pauline snatched her hand away. Goddess, she said, sometimes you are so annoying!

It is my nature, Susannah said, and laughed.

I have learned a thing or two from you, too, said Lily Paul, after several minutes of silence.

Oh, said Susannah, becoming serious.

Yes, said Lily Paul. True education is never a one-way street.

Ouch! said Susannah.

Oh yes, said Lily Paul. I can study just as hard as you. And what I've learned from our years of mutual cramming is that I can neither have you nor be you. Nor can I have your childhood instead of my own. I'm stuck with who I am, she said, twirling a silver lock with her finger. I'm trying to learn that that's not so bad.

Not so bad! laughed Susannah. Not so bad! Darling, it's wonderful! You're gorgeous, rich, a great lover, and a very good cook. What else is there?

A life with you, said Lily Paul, stubbornly.

Susannah sat calmly, smiling into Lily Paul's eyes.

A life with me would be like living with the wind.

Blow, said Lily Paul.

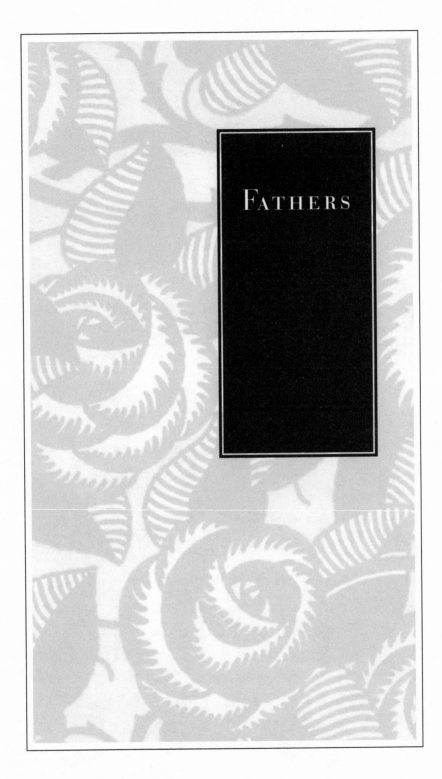

FATHERS

The Cathedral
of the Future

The cathedral of the future will be nature, Señor, said Manuelito. In the end, people will be driven back to trees. To streams. To rocks that do not have anything built on them. That is what the Mundo believe.

This was the boy who might have been my son-in-law. Why had I been so stupid as to divert the stream of life? I might have had grandchildren who grew up to walk thoughtfully about the world teaching these things!

No one among the Mundo believes there is anyone on earth who truly knows anything about why we are here, Señor. Even to have an idea about it would require a very big brain. A computer. That is why, instead of ideas, the Mundo have stories.

You are saying, are you not, I said to Manuelito, that stories have more room in them than ideas?

He laughed.

That is correct, Señor. It is as if ideas are made of blocks. Rigid and hard. And stories are made of a gauze that is elastic. You can almost see through it, so what is beyond is tantalizing. You can't quite make it out; and because the imagination is always moving forward, you yourself are constantly stretching. Stories are the way spirit is exercised.

But surely you people have ideas! I said.

Of course we do. But we know that there is a limit to them. After that, story!

He had told me he must go away for a while. In his absence I must practice the initiation song. I was puzzled by the last stanza, the one that ends "por la luz de los ojos de mi padre."

No, no, Señor, said Manuelito. You keep saying by the light of my father's *eyes*. That is not correct. It is "por la luz de la *sonrisa* de mi padre"! By the light of my father's *smile*.

I shrugged. It seems only natural, I said. The eyes have light, I said. The teeth do not.

Think of the smile as the crescent moon, he said, high in the night sky. Though turned sideways to North Americans, in our hemisphere it is turned like a bowl, or a boat, so that it is like a smile in a dark face, is it not?

Oh, I said. I had never really thought about the moon.

Do not worry, Señor. All you need to do is practice. When the time comes, you will understand.

Why must you go away? I asked.

Remember how I told you that everyone who dies has two tasks? Well, the one that I have to do that does not involve you and Magdalena is in Vietnam.

I realized what this might mean for him. I held out my arms. I am sorry, I said, embracing him.

Do not be sorry for me, Señor. After all, I am safely dead. And as you see, it is not a bad life. But in Vietnam there is a child, a little girl whose spirit died the moment her parents were killed. She is now a prostitute on the streets of Da Nang, and dying of AIDS.

Did you murder her parents? I asked.

I did, he said, simply. After I hid her in a granary basket, through whose chinks she apparently peeked. Our orders were to destroy the village. We destroyed it.

How will you face her? I asked.

She will die, and then it will be easy.

But she will hate you, I said.

No, he said. She will understand immediately that I am bringing back something she has lost. It is what she most wants to take with her into her death.

What is that? I asked.

The moment just before her parents were shot. The last moment of being herself. The last moment of being whole. Of having a soul. It is amazing, is it not, to think that that moment is one we shared? We two, alone of all the world. Complete strangers. Neither speaking the other's language, except through the eyes. And yet, I saved her because she reminded me of Magdalena, the first day we met, the day she stepped on my foot.

Manuelito laughed.

How can you laugh! I asked.

Oh, Señor, he said. Laughter isn't even the other side of tears. It is tears turned inside out. Truly the suffering is great, here on earth. We blunder along, shredded by our mistakes, bludgeoned by our faults. Not having a clue where the dark path leads us. But on the whole, we stumble along bravely, don't you think?

And so you laugh, I said.

I laugh, he said, waving his hand in the air, attempting to disguise a tear.

Bears

Susannah is lounging in a deck chair on the deck of Irene's yacht. She is wearing a red, scoop-neck T-shirt and dark green shorts that close along the side with black buttons. On her feet are white espadrilles. Her hair has grown longer since she's been traveling with Irene, and is in glossy, silver-streaked locks that resemble Pauline's; her left nostril sports a twinkling golden stud; her lanky frame seems deeply bronze against the khaki of the chair. She is reading a letter from Pauline:

The first thing that happens to women after they've seen how being with one another can work, is that they have a case of the frights. It is as if they look into each other's eyes and discover they've been trasformed into bears.

My daughter smiles at this image, enjoys this turn of her former (she thinks) lover's mind, and looks out on a glass-smooth sea. She only misses Pauline when she doesn't hear from her. This puzzles her. The minute she gets a letter, she feels she doesn't miss her at all. But now she thinks: Is this simply a part of being, and of perceiving, the bear? She holds the letter in such a way that it shades her eyes from the sun.

I miss you, the letter continued. Shamelessly. I think about you all the time. Every minute of the day. In fact, I create extra minutes in the day in which to miss you. In my derangement, I have created a new dessert, a completely healthy and delicious blackberry shortcake. Its name is "Oh, Susannah!" Diners are in love! Susannah stretches her arms above her head and inadvertently smells her armpits. She imagines Pauline's head, her silver locks, nestled there. Startled, she blinks her eyes.

It is never smooth sailing, she read. Whether with woman, or, as I imagine, with man. In fact, one of my friends tells me that the surest way to have sympathy for a man is to start sleeping with women. Did you think I would be problem free? Better than Petros? More soulful than that other guy you never liked to talk about? I have problems. I work on them. What more can anyone do?

At this, Susannah sat up. It was time for lunch, and she saw Irene coming toward her.

Did you notice that the boat has stopped? asked Irene, as one of the crew laid out bowls and salad forks.

Has it? asked Susannah, in a daze. She was still thinking of Pauline, and, in fact, mentally writing a response to her which she would later wire from the office-study Irene had thoughtfully set up for her on the astonishingly well-run and self-sufficient boat. She was stuck on one line, the most honest she would ever bring herself to write: You are a bear; I am a bear; yes, I am afraid.

It is over there, just by that outcropping of rocks, that I will place my mother, said Irene, pointing at a sloping hillside that seemed to be sliding into the sea, and on which yellow grasses and bright windflowers winked in the sun. No matter how much sun Irene got, she never seemed to tan. Now she squinted in the direction she pointed, her skin as white as paper and mottled by brown liver spots.

Ah, said Susannah, seeming to relax into the spectacular view. It is stunning. What a view she will have!

Yes, said Irene, mopping up goat cheese and salad juices with a piece of bread. It is not a bad place to spend eternity.

Eternity. The word made Susannah think, quite firmly, of the moment. The moment in which she sat immersed in the daughterly intentions of Irene. Every once in a while, lately, perhaps because she was getting older, she had these moments that seemed dense and deep, true and eternal. They seemed outside of and beyond time, somehow. And in this particular moment, she was languorous from the stately, nearly imperceptible roll of the boat, the excellent grilled fish and opulent Greek salad, the ticklish white wine, and the face of her friend, as Irene looked at the Greek island landscape and straight into her abused and rejected mother's heart.

You see, it is not too far from my former prison, said Irene.

Sure enough, just to the right, but much closer to the sea, sat the small white church. Only now it was surrounded by other buildings that housed a nursery, a hospital, a school, a center for women. The church itself had been transformed into a place where people could learn ancient rituals that had once been beloved by the people of Greece. They involved dancing and prayer as one. Eating and prayer as one. Loving and prayer as one.

It is so different, now, from what it was, said Irene. For one thing, I had a giant fireplace built in one end. A fireplace you can cook in. To me, that is what is always missing from churches.

Fire? asked Susannah.

Of course, said Irene.

Plenty of brimstone, though, said Susannah, laughing.

Being Saved

My daughter is dreaming about her fear of where life is taking her. In the dream, there are two women, each of whom offers her food. She begins to eat the food, happily. Enjoying it. When the first woman sees this, she slowly begins to pour salt over everything. Susannah turns hopefully to the food offered by the other woman. That woman calmly pours a fine stream of sand.

She sits next day with Irene and tells her this dream.

Irene has her tarot deck and lays out the cards.

In one, there is a woman cutting off another woman's hair.

The woman whose hair is being cut is oblivious to what is going on. She is looking into a large mirror that does not show what is being done to her. She likes her reflection so much that she smiles. Not noticing the other woman's frown.

Oh, says Irene, the muddled territory of the blissfully deluded.

Oh, shit, says Susannah, peering at the cards. At least I recognize myself.

You are so deluded it's a wonder you're such an honest person, says Irene.

That's the way I fight my delusions, I think, says Susannah.

Another card that Irene studies shows a woman riding a large elephant. She thinks she is in control, but the elephant is about to step over a boulder that will dislodge her. By the elephant's side, very small, there is a woman yelling up at her, attempting to warn her of the danger. The rider is too into her power trip, however, to hear. Luckily, just at the edge of the card, there appears the tiniest wing of an angel. Not even a whole angel yet, just the promise of one. If the woman comes to her senses, she will be saved.

What does it mean, being saved? asks Susannah.

I think it means becoming aware. Irene pokes out her lips in concentration, reading the cards. And what this card says is that you are gaining that possibility.

Thank goodness, says Susannah.

Your dream is about your sister, the giant one you told me about, said Irene.

Magdalena? asked Susannah, suddenly sitting very straight.

Yes. And it is trying to draw your attention to her resemblance to Pauline.

What? asked Susannah, blinking.

Irene shrugged. I never had a lover myself, but I have known many. Read cards for them. They are always falling in love with members of their own family.

But that's grotesque, said Susannah.

Irene had started to puff on a small (rolled just for her, by order, in Cuba) *cohiba* cigar. As she spoke, she blew smoke from the corner of her mouth.

There is a place where your sister and your lover meet, absolutely.

Susannah thought of the truculent Magdalena, the sensuous Pauline. Where, she snorted, in the world is that?

Right in the middle of your life.

¿Cómo?

Didn't you tell me that Pauline wanted your childhood; that she yearned for the life she assumed you had?

Yes, said Susannah, puzzled.

And even as adults, didn't she try to take it from you by spoiling the times you spent together that were supposed to make up for what she hadn't had?

Susannah thought of the trips, nearly always disastrous, that she had gone on with Pauline. Kalimasa came back to her in all its sultry despair. Pauline running about the countryside like a teenager, ignorant as any ghetto youth of the ancient mores of the culture, stuck on herself and pretending to be stuck on half the young boys she met.

This was your second childhood, too, said Irene. She spoiled it for you.

And yet, thought Susannah, just like my parents' lovemaking, sex with Pauline had somehow brought it back. The feeling of being a child, doing something naughty, and getting away with it in a magical land.

Susannah, said Irene smiling, you are so deluded, so unsure of what exactly is happening, that you do not even recognize your own abuse, your own suffering. You think everyone else has it harder than you do. No wonder these two women in your life have wanted to hit you over the head.

Tears sprang to Susannah's eyes.

No, no, said Irene, clucking like a mother hen and taking her hand. *I* do not want to join them in hitting you over the head. I am an old, old woman, and I understand. You have suffered a spirit fracture. I am the angel, perhaps, who has arrived to help it be, at last, properly set.

A *spirit* fracture? asked Susannah hoarsely, feeling the label fit her wound exactly, and beginning to weep.

Yes, said Irene. Just a fracture. Your spirit is not broken, as was your sister's.

How does Magdalena fit into this? she asked Irene, sniffling.

Irene laughed. Pauline was the woman pouring sand, she said. Even you were able to sense something wrong there. Magdalena was the one pouring salt. In itself, salt is a condiment; it belongs in food. That is why you hardly noticed until it was too late.

Too late? said Susannah.

Yes. At many different points you might have reconnected with your father, but there was a shaker of salt right by your elbow. Before you knew it, in all kinds of ways, Magdalena had unpalatably overseasoned your food. A word here, a whisper there. It should be a crime to be younger than anyone else in a family. If they want to, those who are older can feed you such distortions and lies!

Susannah lay back against the deck chair, sighing, feeling exhausted.

I still don't see the connection between Pauline and Magdalena, she said, queasily. Even the idea of them having something in common caused her to feel slightly incestuous. She thought she must soon heave herself from the deck chair, reel over to the boat's railing, and throw up.

Here, said Irene, seeing her go green around the gills, have this leaf of mint to chew.

The very thing they hated you for having, said Irene, they both tried to steal from you.

My childhood?

Yes, said Irene. But beyond that, your placid happiness itself.

Argh! said Susannah, flinging herself up from her chair and off, at a lurch, toward the sea.

You are on a boat! Up very high! Irene called after her. Don't forget!

Susannah had forgotten, actually.

Now she leaned, gagging, over the railing, caught by it, held by it, kept by it from falling perhaps to her death. And kept from falling as well by the voice of Irene. Her odd little *watti-tuu*, angel, come to life.

But I wanted them to have happiness, too! she wailed, as she sank to her knees and a level that permitted her large head to rest in Irene's small arms. Why couldn't they see that, and leave mine alone!

You were born with yours, and somehow managed to keep it, said Irene, softly. That is why to others it appeared you never rebelled. Even going against the grain made you happy. Being naughty and even being punished for it made you smile! This is sometimes enough to make an enemy of anyone.

What? asked Susannah, who hadn't heard.

Irene flipped the nub of her cigar through the railing and into the sea. Then very carefully she dried Susannah's tears with a bit of the sleeve of her nubby white linen cardigan.

I said, Fuck them, she said.

And yet, inexplicably, in the very next morning's post, rowed out to Irene's yacht in a decrepit dinghy whose oars creaked with an ancient sound, there was a large, carefully wrapped parcel from Pauline. Susannah unwrapped it slowly, with hesitation and distrust at what she would find, and then stared in amazement at a clear gallon-size plastic jar filled to the brim with green-apple jellybeans.

Crossing Over

I do not know
where I've
come from
I do not know
where I go
I only know
that I feel
in my heart
that I am here
surprised
a very small part
of *Love*.

It is time, Señor.

Manuelito had come back and had been observing me as I practiced the last stanza of the Mundo initiation song.

Are you ready? he asked.

Ah, Manuelito, I said, opening my arms to embrace him. How radiant you look! Even more than you did before. I am ready, I said, with your help.

He smiled.

Did everything go well, where you were? I asked.

Everything went very well, Señor. The young woman I harmed is freed to do the work of her own two tasks.

But she was just a child when the harm was done to her, I said, surely she can't be blamed for whatever hurt she caused others later on.

It does not seem to work that way, Señor. It seems we are responsible for everything we do, no matter how the chain of events began.

But is this right? I asked. Is it fair?

Manuelito shrugged.

We were standing now on the side of a mountain, looking out over a valley. Sweeping down the hillside and into the valley, through which a glinting river flowed, there were millions of blue wildflowers. It was breathtakingly beautiful, and I recognized it at once.

We are back in the mountains! I cried.

Yes, said Manuelito.

Your homeland!

Yes, he said again.

Are we near my old house? I asked, turning to scan the area.

No, Señor, not near your house, but near mine. Mine and Magdalena's.

Yours, I stammered, and Magdalena's!

Sí, he said.

I looked all around. There was no house.

It is here, he said, with humble pride, stepping behind a bush and into a cave.

It was a tiny space. An old blanket lay on the floor. A large clay pot with a lid stood beside a rock. The floor was smooth as if freshly swept. Through the branches of the shrub that guarded the door I looked out into a dazzling drift of blue flowers that grew so densely that by the time they reached the valley and spread across it they appeared to have turned into the sea.

Yes, said Manuelito. When Magdalena and I used to be here we would look out, just as you are doing, and imagine floating away on a big boat.

This is a part of the ceremony? I asked.

Yes, said Manuelito. The week or so before the marriage of their children, the Mundo believe it is right for the young man to invite the young woman's father into the space that will be her home. It is important that he see what view she will have, so that he can imagine the growing spaciousness of her heart; it is important that he see where she will live; where she will be loved; where she will lie.

And her mother? I asked.

That ceremony comes even earlier; it would have happened the week before. You can see that the women have already been here. The floor is swept, there is water in the water jar. The blanket is spread out on the floor. You and I will gather firewood and find food. Or you and I would have done so, he said.

Manuelito cleared his throat.

Is it satisfactory to you, Señor? he asked.

Years ago, of course, it would not have been. This hovel, I would have scoffed. This *cave*?

It is perfect, my son, I said.

If it is okay, he said, we can begin.

—

From a distance I could see something, someone moving. Nearer, I saw it was a woman, riding a black horse. Nearer still, I saw that it was Magdalena. Not Magdalena the twisted, Magdalena the furious and obese, Magdalena the grotesque. But Magdalena as she was before she began to eat so much. Magdalena the tall and supple, Magdalena the self-possessed, both willful and serene. She was incredibly beautiful; and I was shocked to think I'd never really noticed this. Her skin was very dark, the color, truly, of chocolate. Bittersweet. Her eyes very large and daring; her "big" head of hair wild as the wind. She was wearing a low-cut, very white blouse; her full green skirt was hitched up so that her thighs gleamed in the sun. It was as if I had never seen her ride before; she and the horse were one.

For a long time I watched her approach, moving very fast, but arriving very slowly.

I looked at Manuelito, whose eyes were devoted solely to the approach of my daughter, his whole face shining with love. So bright was his whole being that I felt almost burned by it, and had to look away.

There is something that I think I forgot to tell you, Señor, he said.

What is that? I asked.

It is about the five places that are kissed.

Yes? I said.

There are actually more than that. Seeing Magdalena made me remember them.

What are they? I asked.

They are the palms of the hands, because our hands serve us faithfully always. And our feet, because they carry us to our destiny. They are kissed on the arch, he added. He looked caressingly toward my daughter thundering toward us on her black horse, deliberately arriving in slow motion, I realized, for his, and her, enjoyment of the moment. It was taking so long I thought I'd make a joke.

Will she ever actually get here? I asked.

Manuelito laughed.

Not before you are ready, he said, soberly.

I'm ready, I said.

No, he said. I also forgot to explain one other thing. And that is about the light.

The light? I asked. Looking about me and realizing there was a lot of it.

Yes, he said. Remember how we kiss all the places that let in the light? And remember how you didn't understand about the moon?

Moonlight, I said. I got it.

No, Señor, that is not quite it.

I don't got it? I said, jokingly.

No. And it is a rather long story, now that I think of it.

My daughter looks pretty eager to be here, I said.

She is eager to be here, to be with me and with you. But she will not come before we're ready. Please, he said, help me not to fail at my job.

Okay, I said.

In the first place, he said, you should know that my mother and father have already welcomed Magdalena, so she is really coming home. She has been kissed everywhere with much tenderness; her breasts have been blessed. This would have been done when the moon was full, and my father's part would have been done after the kissing and the blessing. But my mother's part would have involved telling Magdalena the story of woman and the moon. Of how woman is connected to it and shares its rhythms. That a woman's tides, her blood tides, connect with the moon. That this is how women know in their bodies that they are a part of everything, even something so distant as the moon.

But how are men to know this? asked Manuelito, looking pensively at me.

It was my turn to shrug.

The Mundo thought long about this question, he said. And they studied the sky for a sign that they, those who were men, were connected also. You know how much we hate to be left out! He laughed.

Why do you laugh? I asked.

Because it was right there all the time!

What? I asked.

The moon! he said. The very same moon. Finally, after who knows how many millennia, they got it. And this, Manuelito said, still smiling, is what they finally got. A woman, living in nature, is full when the moon is full, no? And if a lot of women live together, they and the moon are full at the same time; when the moon releases and begins to wane, that is when they release their blood. It is powerful, this connection, no? Now, during this time, a man may not make love to a woman. She feels somewhat irritable, somewhat messy, though she does not mind, since she and the moon are sharing, as they say, a big moment. But for sure there is a period in there when woman just naturally does not want to be bothered! I remember that my mother, during such times, would actually throw things at my father!

Ah, Manuelito, I said with regret, what an idiot I feel not to have really gotten to know them.

Señora Robinson knew them, he said. She and my mother were rather alike. Anyway, he said, there is a period of recovery from the "big moment" that women have had with the moon, when men are unsure how or whether they will be received; then there is a period when sexual contact must be avoided unless one wants children, and every Mundo person knows we cannot support very many. We love to make love, though, so we are somewhat gloomy during this time. Manuelito pantomimed this condition, the corners of his mouth turned down. Then, he said, there is the dark of the moon, when not a whole lot is happening *either*! But *then*, he said, brightening, just when the men have given up hope, the moon appears again. And in our eyes, it appears as a smile! Very tentative at first, but pretty soon, a wide grin! For by now the women are totally receptive. It is a good time to make love!

Manuelito laughed merrily. We are so relieved, Señor! And this, the Mundo believe, is man's connection to the moon. The crescent moon, which is sometimes like a bowl or a boat, is the moon smiling its light on the good lovemaking that is to come! The moon, while forever a woman, for just a little while becomes, also, a man! (That is why, when you spoke to us about a man in the moon, it was not a foreign concept.)

If you are in love, and going to meet your lover, to make love, you think of the moon as a father, happily looking down on you. For Mundo fathers *are* happy that their children, the girls as well as the boys, enjoy what your culture calls sex. And that is why a young girl sings, as she goes to her lover, just as does a young boy: "by the light of my father's smile!" And that is why no one among the Mundo would marry when the moon is full, but only when it has waned and then reappears, as a smile in a dark face, in the sky!

I finally got it. That this was what my poor daughter had been singing about, all those years ago! "Por la luz . . . por la luz . . ." I could still hear her despairing cry. There had been an element of pleading in her song that I had ignored. She had been begging me to see, to witness, the light that she had found. To love and bless what she loved. But I had refused. I had brought her to a culture and a people I'd claimed to respect. She had fallen in love with them, and been betrayed when I myself stopped short. When I myself, in her eyes, had regressed.

She had been flying across the mountain slopes on the back of the shining black stallion before us, secure among these "alien" people, yearning body and soul for the shelter and passion of Manuelito's arms, believing that the moon was with her, and so perhaps her own father might be. But she was, unfortunately, the daughter of a fool. I had failed her and without reason destroyed her life.

Manuelito, I said, I wish I were dead.

Ah, you are now ready, Señor, he said.

—

In the blink of an eye, the black stallion, Vado, reared in our faces, and a triumphant Magdalena jumped from his back.

Fathers

My name is Father, I said to her, when I found myself looking into her eyes. I am the father watching over you, the daughter that I love. She appeared mutely humble, hearing this, for so ebullient a soul. Her gratitude so raw that had I felt it in life, I am sure it would have made me bleed.

When the time came, and I knelt before her, I kissed not only her palms and the arches of her feet, which seemed to buzz with energy, but also her knees. Because, after all, it is to our knees that we must sometimes be driven, before we can recognize, witness, or welcome our own light.

Light

It was like Susannah to die of old age, at home, in bed, in her sleep, and while dreaming!

Of what were you dreaming? I asked her, as we watched the gathering of her friends, some with plates of food in their hands, coming into her house and into her room.

Oh, she said, smiling, I was dreaming of Anand, and the way that we met.

Anand?

Yes, she said. He is the man in the corner, with the wonderful white mustache, weeping. He is also the brother of the man I married. You recall Petros, no?

Believe me, the recollection is vague by now, I said.

She laughed.

I met Anand the day we disinterred the body of Irene's mother and reburied it on a hillside overlooking the sea.

Susannah's had been a life that, to my regret, and because of my own need to cause her suffering, I knew little about, no matter that the Mundo thought the dead knew everything. Curious, I urged her to continue.

Oh, it is a long story, she said, but we have a long time. I will tell it to you. By the time she got to the digging up of the trunk in which Irene's nameless mother was buried, I was almost in tears.

Her mother's trunk was just like the one at the foot of my bed, she said, inviting me, with a gesture, to look. Petros sold that one to me for a dollar and twenty kisses. He was ashamed of it because it was crude. But, in fact, it was crude only because he did not understand its value.

And what was that? I said, peering more critically at the large cedar chest with carved flowers and mountains and rivers all over it. While I looked, a very old woman, even older-looking than my sister, with snowy dreadlocks to her knees, sank down upon the trunk, weeping.

Ah, said Susannah, Pauline. Is there nothing I can do to solace her?

The only way to solace anyone who loved you in life is to be a good memory, I said.

No kidding, she said, reflectively.

It is large, I said, imagining Petros dragging the heavy trunk all the way from Greece.

Yes, said Susannah. And for good reason. In the old days the trunk or chest contained everything a young woman took with her when she married and left her parents' house. It contained linen and silver, her clothes, her small spindle, even her cooking pots and pans. By attaching two curved pieces of wood underneath, that fit neatly inside the trunk when not in use, its owner could turn it into a cradle. During her marriage, and after her babies were big, she kept everything she valued inside it. When she died, she was buried in it.

And so, I said, Irene's mother was buried in her portable coffin!

Or in her cradle, said Susannah.

—

On the low, simple wooden bed, Susannah wore a long green nightgown, beautifully embroidered. Her thin white hair was in a dozen plaits with red ribbon wrapped around them, and rested on her chest. In one hand was a feather, in the other a green jellybean. Several of her friends, who appeared haggard, as if they'd sat with her all night, were slowly beginning to stir. Anand rose from his vigil in the corner and approached the bed.

At first I thought he was Petros, said Susannah, looking tenderly at him. They resemble each other so much. I think I thought so all the while I watched him and the other men digging up Irene's mother's body. But then, when we were having the ceremony of reburial, and he joined the women dancing, I realized it couldn't be. He was dancing and weeping, right along with us!

He weeps a lot, I said.

He's so heavy! she said. It's true. When we got to know each other and became lovers and then just good, comfortable old friends, I used to listen to his stories about his work among the poor and among battered women and children and in the refugee camps—apparently there are always refugee camps in Greece—and I would think how his deep concern for people, his taking on of moral burdens, which meant he could never abandon Greece, made Petros seem like Anand Lite.

She laughed. One too light, the other too heavy, she said.

And Pauline just right?

With time, yes, she said. She needed only to honor her own sovereignty and to relearn tenderness.

She should get up off the trunk, I said, so that they can put you in it.

My trunk is my house, she said. But I do care a great deal for the one Petros sold me. His mother gave it to him, even though he was a boy, because she lost all her daughters while they were babies. He lugged it off to America, but was eager to get rid of it. I had an instinct that it would have a history I would uncover someday.

Susannah did not seem at all surprised that we were having this conversation in the same room in which she lay dead.

No, she said, reading my thoughts, nothing surprises me anymore. Once you've smelled an orange or really seen a tree, what could surprise you?

Poor Irene, I said, thinking of her small friend.

She wanted to see her mother's face, said Susannah. I thought it was probably not a good idea. Anand thought it was not. But she insisted. That meant opening the trunk.

She sighed.

And? I asked.

They had bound her mother's hands and feet. She was all in black. They had placed a black shroud over her head.

Black is beautiful, I said, sarcastically.

When it is the truth, yes, said Susannah. That was its only beauty in this situation.

And Irene?

She died within the month.

No, I said.

Susannah shrugged. She was old, and frail, she said sadly. Sighing, she continued. She was so small, so alone, so fierce, so loving, and her people did everything they could to hurt her. It is beyond belief.

It is a woman's life, I said.

As we watched, Susannah's friends began to cover her bed, and her body, with the boughs of trees. I looked around the small room where she lay.

I thought you'd have a more splendid house, I said.

My splendid house was crushed by an even more splendid tree, she replied. I learned to live, contentedly, in the lesson I was taught by that loss.

Aren't you curious about why I am here? I asked. Or about our parents, or Manuelito?

As she was pondering this, I thought of all of them.

Of teaching my savvy mother how to cross the river. Of the way I felt when my father blessed me. After the blessing, he simply vanished. I was left alone with Manuelito. We kissed. We were still kissing when I found myself in Susannah's room watching her die. From the look of things, especially from the look of Susannah's white hair and very old body, decades had passed. This meant, had to mean, that Manuelito was also gone.

Remember, Magdalena, Manuelito had told me, that it is true, as the Mundo believe, that eternity is forever. But at the same time, it is only as long as there is need.

Our eternity together had been long and blissful. Now it was over. Like any other love affair. This thought made me laugh.

What's the joke? asked Susannah.

What's not the joke? I replied.

—

Looking more closely at the contents of my sister's room, I saw that there were stacks and piles of papers and books. Notebooks of all colors and sizes. Copies of her published books, videos, recordings of her readings. Her friends were slowly and methodically pouring oil over everything.

When it burns, said Susannah, it will smell of frankincense. She seemed delighted, like a child in anticipation of a marshmallow roast.

You can't mean what I think you mean, I said, as we watched every person, even the little children, bring in more dry twigs, branches of fir trees, dead leaves, and straw.

She nodded.

But, Susannah, I said, this is your legacy!

Magdalena, she said, you are here because you are sorry you deliberately led me astray such a very long time ago. That is all the legacy I need.

But you won't be remembered, I said, somewhat desperately for a ghost.

It is the need to be remembered that has caused most of the trouble in the world, she said. Most of the conquering. Destruction of what is natural. War.

Well, your books are in libraries, I said. So your gesture is symbolic.

Yes, she said. Unfortunately.

Only her face and her hands were now visible, underneath everything that had been piled on top of her. Her friends came slowly forward, a final time, to touch her and to say good-bye. Finally only Anand and Pauline remained. With a look at Anand, Pauline left the room. Out of respect, while he knelt beside Susannah, his old bones creaking, I looked away. Soon Pauline returned, and Anand left the room. Again, I looked away. When next I looked, it was to see that Susannah's body was alone in the room, and that Pauline had cut off and left, draped across the mound of dry straw, fir branches, and leaves, the full length of her dreadlocked white hair.

The flames from her burning house were bright and reminded me of a poem:

When life descends into the pit
I must become my own candle
willingly burning myself
to light up the darkness around me.

Acknowledgments

I thank the spirit of Eros for its presence in my life and for the lessons it has taught me. I thank the community of spiritual helpers who gathered to support me during the writing of this book. Among them I thank Barbara G. Walker for her immensely important scholarship, and especially for her profound and indispensable book *The Woman's Encyclopedia of Myths and Secrets.* I thank Isabel Fonseca for her clear-hearted, insightful, and heroic book *Bury Me Standing: The Gypsies and Their Journey.* I thank Frans De Waal and Frans Lanting for introducing me, in their book *Bonobo: The Forgotten Ape,* to cousins I had imagined, and written about in an earlier novel, but without proof of their actual existence. I thank the men and women who came to consciousness during the Vietnam War—including Ron Kovic and Oliver Stone—and who returned to tell us what happened to them there. I thank the people of Mexico for having, over the centuries, taken in small wave upon small wave of Indians and African-Amerindians fleeing genocide and enslavement in the United States. These were some of our best people; it is profoundly moving to see in Mexico today, in the eyes of their descendants, these freedom-loving ancestors looking back at me. I thank Zelie Kūli-aikanu'u Duvauchelle for inviting me to share life-changing adventures and for loving her Hawaiian ancestors so much she has learned to sing their songs. I thank Peter Bratt and Benjamin Bratt for being an inspiration. I thank Wynton Marsalis for loving our soul. I thank the Great Spirit of the Universe for regularly carrying me to the edge, permitting me to contemplate the drop, and for holding me well. *Ho!*

—ALICE WALKER
Temple Jook House, Mendocino, California
June 1997

ABOUT THE AUTHOR

ALICE WALKER won the Pulitzer Prize and the National Book Award for her novel *The Color Purple*. Her many other bestselling books include *Possessing the Secret of Joy* and *The Temple of My Familiar*. She is the author of five novels, two collections of short stories, three collections of essays, five volumes of poetry, and several children's books. Her books have been translated into more than two dozen languages. Born in Georgia, Alice Walker now lives in Northern California.

A NOTE ON THE TYPE

This book was set in Fairfield, the first typeface from the hand of the distinguished American artist and engraver Rudolph Ruzicka (1883–1978).

Rudolph Ruzicka was born in Bohemia and came to America in 1894. He set up his own shop, devoted to wood engraving and printing, in New York in 1913 after a varied career working as a wood engraver, in photoengraving and banknote printing plants, and as an art director and free-lance artist. He designed and illustrated many books, and was the creator of a considerable list of individual prints—wood engravings, line engravings on copper, and aquatints.